His Regency Goddess

STEFFY SMITH

Steffy Smith Books

First published in Australia in September 2024 by Steffy Smith

Text copyright © Steffy Smith, 2024

Edited by Juicy Details Romance Editing, 2024

Cover Art by Holly Perret, The Swoonies Romance Book Design

A catalogue record for this book is available from the National Library of Australia.

ISBN (Print '25') 978-1-7637632-3-4

ISBN (E-book '24') 978-0-6454448-7-2

 Formatted with Vellum

All my gratitude

Alivia – thank you for sharing this opportunity that allowed me to put my hand up. And of course, for being a beta reader. Your insights were invaluable and any mention of 'hands' will remind me of you.

Gloria – forever in your debt. The second time you have beta-read for me which I am so very, very thankful for. Your 'eye' for historical romance is incomparable!

Monica & Maria – what a joy working with you was. Words cannot express how over the moon I am with your polishing touches to His Regency Goddess!

Never Forget

You are enough.
If you want to believe in something, believe in that.
xxx

A little bit of Sin...

Who is this Goddess?
"Daniel?"
"Yes Sin?"
"Please tell me your wife is the blonde."

Contents

Chapter One

London, 1818

Sophie stood in front of the mirror at Mrs Bean's Magazin des Modes on 32 Albemarle Street and sighed. She could not help comparing her figure to the waif like women of the ton. According to Margot, this modiste was the talk of society. Sophie was here for the season to vie for an unattached gentleman; one that would appreciate her fuller figure and fill her life with passion. Her first step had been a new wardrobe, and it was barely completed in time, following weeks of fittings The stress and expense felt justified as she tried the outfits on one by one; they slipped over her curves like well- tailored gloves.

Sophie had never had a season as a debutante. Her parents, the Earl and Countess of Stockdon, had arranged her marriage at eight and ten years of age to a duke almost twenty years her senior. She simply went from Sophia Whitelaw to Sophia Westcott. Neither name felt like her true self. She preferred to be called Sophie or Margot's lifelong moniker for her, 'Soph'. When her parents informed her of her impending marriage, her first thought was that at least her monogrammed accessories could remain the same. It was a marriage of convenience that had lasted six years, followed by one year of mourning. The mourning had seemed to last much longer than the years of marriage and, sinful as it felt, she was ready to start her own life. So much had changed in the last seven years. Her personality, her body, her needs, and her wants were now her own to control. This was the time when Sophie would take her life in her own hands and make choices that gave her pleasure. Like the arts. She wanted to explore, appreciate, and collect beautiful objects of her own.

Sophie ran her hands along the dip of her waist, the Pomona green satin dress she had commissioned by the modiste clung to her curves in flattering lines. She had rejected the current high-waisted trend knowing it did not suit her figure and was pleased she had taken such a bold step. Sophie was excited to display her womanly figure to its fullest potential. Her mother always told her that she had childbearing hips. The irony was that, after years of marriage, she had never been with child. Sophie had designed the dress to accentuate her bust and hips and the soft bulge of her belly, allowing the material to "ow from her hips instead of hanging straight down from her bosom. *My build is not petite, but by dressing to my shape I am now going to embrace who I am, not try to fit in with society women.*

She felt someone watching her, and she looked up to see Margot's smiling reflection in the mirror. Margot had graciously taken Sophie in for the season, or forever as she kept telling her. They had spent many a late night giggling and talking like silly girls rather than a married mother of two and a widow.

"What is making you smile so?" Sophie asked with an arched brow.

"You are exuding confidence. You look amazing and I love

that you know it, Soph," Margot told her with an excited clap of her hands.

"I feel amazing. I was so uncertain about how these designs would turn out. I have spent so much time comparing myself to others that I forgot to appreciate my own unique self."

Sophie tried to ignore the taunting voice in her mind telling her to stop being vain. She had been trying to shift the balance in the battle between her inner critic and her inner heroine. It was exhausting at times but with perseverance, her inner heroine had been making great strides in overcoming her self-doubt.

"You have always been beautiful Soph, inside and out." "You are my closest friend. You have to say that," she said with an airy laugh. It was not often anyone called her beautiful, but her inner heroine reminded her to start loving herself for who she was. That included her orange hair and voluptuous figure. Sophie had shared her plan for this season with Margot. After a year of mourning and years of a loveless marriage, she wanted a moment of unabashed passion.

Sophie could not think ill of her late husband; he hadn't been cruel. They had just never had a loving connection, a reality of many arranged marriages amongst the peerage. They had slept in separate rooms with weekly conjugal visits. As duchess, she managed their social activities and the staff of the many houses and manors within his dukedom. That responsibility was now for the new heir and his bride. She had no regrets about handing the role over. She was lucky her late husband had left her an inheritance that included her dowry, so she was a wealthy widow in her own right. What she wanted was love, the love she saw between Margot and her husband, Viscount Daniel Stanford. The looks of unadulterated passion they shared when they thought no one was watching filled her with envy. Sophie wanted to feel the completion of the inkling the weekly visits from her husband had only hinted at.

"You are looking so fierce and determined! Pray tell, what you are thinking?" Margot said.

Taking one last look at her figure, she turned to face Margot and a grin spread across her face. This dress was perfect for this evening's soiree, and it must be a sign that it was completed in time for her to wear tonight.

"I am thinking I shall order many more in this style to prepare for my delayed debut."

Chapter Two

Sinclair Montgomery rubbed his tired eyes. They were dry and itchy and he had forgotten how he hated travelling by godforsaken ship. Throwing his head back, he looked at his surroundings. White's was so comforting. It felt like he had been here the day before with his friends, playing cards, drinking whisky, and trying to one up each other with the sauciest titbit about their latest trysts. That was four years ago. Four long years of travelling. Gambling for the reckless thrill, drinking whisky to drown his sorrows, and tumbling women for moments of bliss so he could briefly forget. Four years ago, he was the younger brother of a future Marquess, content in his role as the second son.

Sinclair had never been as controlled as Andrew and hadn't needed to be. Andrew was clever and shrewd and was meant to do remarkable things. Life, in its cruel way, determined it was not meant to be. Andrew's life was cut short by a freakish accident and Sinclair had spent the next four years trying to understand why. Why did fate choose Andrew's horse to buck him off without warning and not Sinclair, the reckless and foolish younger brother? He had watched in horror as the events unfolded, helpless to stop them playing out before his eyes.

Picking up his glass of whisky, Sinclair threw back the liquid in one gulp as he tried to block out the images. He had not wanted to return home but one of his father's letters had finally caught up with him as he traipsed across Europe. Marquess Maxwell Montgomery was unwell and wanted his heir to return home. Sinclair suspected his father was exaggerating. He was a wily old fox. But the guilt had worked nevertheless, so here he was back in England. He had sent his luggage ahead and sent his best friend Daniel a missive to meet at White's within the hour He hoped to regain his bearings before facing his father. He did not want to be recognised, so he was wearing a heavy coat, a wide brimmed hat pulled low, and a week-old beard. He only revealed his identity to the doorman and found himself one of the dimmer and more private corners of the establishment.

"Look who finished kicking up a lark and came home!" Daniel's gravelly voice coupled with a slap on the back broke up his melancholy thoughts. Seeing his familiar grin gave Sinclair a sense of comfort he had not realised he needed.

"It is good to see you, Daniel. You look well, apart from some lines across your face and grey hairs," Sinclair said with a grin. "Marriage treating you well?"

"To be frank, I don't know why I didn't marry sooner. Why were we so against it? Wait till you meet Margot and my boys," he said proudly. "But that isn't news, Sin. I want to hear about you. Why didn't you tell me you were coming? You are in desperate need of a shave. Are you in hiding? Do you need money?" Daniel asked as he took in Sinclair's appearance.

"No, nothing like that! My father has finally gotten his way. I booked passage and boarded a ship before I had the sense to change my mind. The beard...well, I thought it would be nice to enjoy the last vestiges of neglected nobility. And money? I survived all these years through an ongoing lucky streak of whist."

"Well, I am not ashamed to say I have missed you, Sin. I am really happy to see you. I hope you are home for good?"

"I think I am, as my father claims to be ailing. I will soon find out. I know he wants me to step into Andrew's shoes. Did I do a disservice to his memory, wallowing for so long?" Even though he spoke these words staring into his cup, he could feel Daniel's empathetic gaze upon him.

"I also looked up to Andrew as a big brother. I still miss him. You are doing the right thing. Last I saw your father, he was doing fine, just lonely. He is going to be so happy you are home."

Daniel stood up, pulling Sin with him.

"My townhouse is a few doors down from yours now. Let me give you a ride home. See your father, get washed up, and for the love of God, have a shave. The first event of the season is tonight, and you need to come along with me. My wife Margot has a friend staying with us and I am already discarded in favour of shopping and gossip."

Sin followed him to the carriage where Daniel kept up a constant of stream of conversation and questions. As they pulled into Grosvenor Street, the discussion turned bawdy.

"So, all those women in all those countries, and must have gone through thousands of french letters?" Daniel asked.

"I may have lost all good sense, but I didn't lose my good taste in women", Sin laughed, thinking of the beautiful women he had bedded.

"There is my home," Daniel suddenly pointed out the window. "That is my wife." Two women exited the carriage. One was blonde and petite. The other had fiery hair and was the very definition of voluptuous. Sinclair poked his head out of the window to get a closer look. The women waved back curiously, as they recognised Daniel. The red-haired woman conjured vivid imagery of the ancient statues and paintings he had seen on red clay pots as he travelled through Greece and Italy. A man could only hope to come across one of the beautiful women of myths and legends in his lifetime.

Who is this Goddess?

"Daniel?"

"Yes Sin?"

"Please tell me your wife is the blonde."

Chapter Three

"Margot, is it my imagination or was that man with your husband ogling me?"

Sophie stood frozen in place, mostly flattered but a little concerned. Who was this leering stranger? Was this a compliment or did she look ghastly? She tried to catch her reflection in a window. She tried and failed to conjure a vision of him in her mind, as her brief glimpse of him had only left an impression of his expression, like he wanted something from her. This man had seen something in her.

"I saw it as well. He was indeed ogling you," Margot confirmed with a big grin. "I have no idea who he is or how my husband spent his day. Let's go inside and wait for him. An interrogation is in order!"'

She followed Margot to the parlour and accepted the cup of tea and saucer placed in her hands. Sophie tapped her foot impatiently against the floor as they waited for Daniel to arrive home. The house was in a quiet lull while the children napped. Taking a sip of her tea, she looked to the door again and let out a sigh. *What could possibly be delaying Daniel so?*

"You are so eager to find out who he is. Are you smitten with the ogling stranger?" Margot teased at hearing her sigh.

"No, I was actually thinking how nice and quiet it is when the children are asleep," she teased back. There was no pretence that the children were anything but a boisterous duo.

Margot started a retort but they heard the door closing.

He was home!

Margot stuck her head outside the parlour door and gestured to the viscount. "Come in here and be quiet. The children are asleep, but we have many questions for you, dear husband."

In a moment, Daniel's grinning face appeared as he entered the parlour. He poured himself a cup of tea and took a seat on the cushioned chair next to Margot. Sophie giggled at how quickly he joined them for tea and gossip. She gazed fondly at the blonde and blue-eyed golden couple that ticked all polite society's boxes. Both came from respected families and had now started their own with their two fair-haired boys. "This is about my friend, isn't it?" Daniel asked as he waggled his eyebrows at her.

"Never do that again, you look like a ridiculous fop!" Margot answered, a snort escaping as she mocked him.

"Hush! Do you want those beautiful terrors to awaken?" Daniel said, waving off his wife's jibe. "But I'm correct, am I not?" he added, as he turned to Sophie.

Knowing these two could heartily banter for hours she interjected before either could speak.

"You are correct, I am very curious as to why he looked at me so...so...something?" she finished lamely, not finding the appropriate words to describe the heated gaze.

"He is quite taken with you," Daniel said with a sly smile. "His was a look of pure interest in knowing every detail about you."

"I knew it!" Margot said loudly, which caused her husband to hush her again.

"What did he say? Who is he? Does he like me?" she gushed out, not knowing what to think or ask first. Her stomach fluttered like she had swallowed hundreds of butterflies and they were beating their wings furiously in an effort to escape.

Daniel held up his hands in surrender.

"Let me start from the beginning. His name is Sinclair Montgomery. He is my oldest friend and has returned home today from a long sojourn aboard. He is indeed very much interested in you. To quote Sin he said, 'please tell me the blonde one is your wife' and then proceeded to tell me that you were the most delectable goddess he had ever set his eyes upon."

"Sinclair Montgomery? His reputation as a prolific reprobate has not been forgotten by anyone in the ton, Daniel. Soph cannot tie herself to him!" Margot gasped.

Sinclair Montgomery. Sophie had heard the name and recalled vague rumours, but was unconcerned. Her inner critic was more concerned with asking why a man who could have any woman he wanted would be intrigued by her.

She looked outside the paned window and noted the sun was starting to set. In a few hours, they would attend the first pre-party to the season, an intimate gathering of the most sought-after socialites. Sophie did not make that list, but she would be attending as a guest of Daniel and Margot.

"Will he be at the party tonight?" she asked, interrupting the bickering couple. Daniel insisted Sin was a man changed and grown and Margot scoffed that anyone with that moniker would always be a rakehell. At her question, they both turned to her, Daniel smug and Margot exasperated.

"Surely you are not interested, Soph? You will have so

many men to choose from!" Margot scolded with a sideways look at Daniel.

"He will be there tonight. James is an old friend of Sin's as well and will be very happy to see him." Daniel moved to stand beside Margot. "Do not frown, my love. You can berate me later. I am going to get those rascals up." He bent down to kiss Margot on the forehead.

Sophie watched the exchange, knowing their tiff meant nothing real. Their banter was full of trust and honesty, which is what made them such a great couple.

I want that someday, in my heart of hearts I do.

Chapter Four

S in's old bedroom felt comfortable but also strange. It was like stepping into his old life without realising he had ever left it behind. The reunion with his father had been bittersweet. The man was still strong in mind, but Sin could see he had become frail in body. Sin's long absence meant he could clearly observe the physical changes in his father. His hair was completely grey and thinning, and his build seemed to have shrunk in stature. They shared the same dark eyes, black as sin as his brother had always joked. Andrew had inherited their mother's lighter shade of brown. Sin was relieved the shrewd, albeit sad, look in his father's eyes was still strong.

His father had observed that the fatigue of travel had caught up with him and ushered him to sleep. He told Sin they had all their days to catch up on their lives, his tone brooking no suggestion that Sin had not returned for good. The familiarity of the luxurious mattress and feathered pillow coaxed him into such a deep afternoon slumber he barely recalled anything he may have dreamed.

Luckily he had awoken in time to get ready for the night.

Normally he gave no thought to when he stumbled in to a social event. Tonight it was different. He was eager to see that luscious specimen of perfection named Sophie. He had always appreciated a more voluptuous woman, thick thighs wrapped around him with handfuls of fleshy buttocks he could grab. There were so many women abroad who fulfilled that bill, exotic beauties with sultry accents. But for some reason he could never connect emotionally. He missed the quaint and proper manners of an English miss. His ideal woman would be that, but also wanton behind closed doors, only for him. He recalled many seasons where every woman was either blatantly on the hunt for a husband or married and looking for an a!air. It was predictable and boring. Sophie, though, was widowed, and a woman who hopefully knew what she wanted. And if it was a passionate tryst, he could give it to her. The sight of her at that distance had aroused him; the thought of her up close made him hard as granite. He was tempted to stroke his urges away but abstained, knowing the moment he had her would be made all the more satisfying.

He was nearly dressed and moved to the mirror to don his cravat. Sin crossed the ends of the stiff white cloth around his neck before reaching for a silver and jade pin from his travels to hold the ends in place. Stepping back, he eyed his full length before pulling on his black waistcoat. Black and white with a little pop of colour. His light brown hair and dark eyes contrasted well with the black and white and his bright grin flashed as he took himself in. He believed men that wore colourful clothes were fops. He picked up his gold pocket watch and checked the time before placing it in his trouser pockets. It was half past nine. A perfect time. Not too early, not too late. And he could wait no longer.

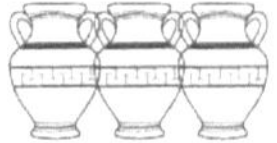

"Look at you, you swell devil!" James Graybridge, the host of the evening, welcomed him with a warm embrace.

"It is good to see you, James," Sin replied as he returned the embrace. James was another close friend, but one he had not kept in contact with as he had Daniel.

James introduced him to his wife Cecily, a petite brunette who was all smiles and giggles. He looked back to James who winked at him over the top of her head. James's ideal woman had always been a giddy deb and it seemed his old friend had landed himself the perfect match.

"Come Sin, let us go and reacquaint ourselves over a drink before you get rushed by all the other guests".

"Good idea. Has Daniel arrived yet?" He hoped his tone was casual and did not betray his eagerness at seeing Sophie.

"He has, with his wife and her friend. Let me get him as well. We three can share a drink just like old times."

James asked Cecily to bring Daniel over and in moments Daniel, his wife, and that delectable Goddess were walking towards him. Sophie was wearing a green dress, the colour setting o! her ginger hair and accentuating those pale-green doe eyes. She seemed nervous, with a wide-eyed innocent look. He watched the tip of her tongue escape and lick her plump pink lips. His eyes narrowed as he noticed he was not the only one admiring Sophie. His body tensed as jealousy surged through him.

Get it together Sin, he scolded himself. He sensed a hostile stare and shifted his gaze to find the narrowed eyes of Daniel's wife.

"Sin, is this an improved you, arriving at a party so early?" Daniel ribbed. "Allow me the pleasure of introducing my wife, my Viscountess Margot, and her dear friend Dowager Duchess of Whitmore, Sophia Westcott. This is my old friend Lord Sinclair Montgomery." Daniel and James appeared to be a few drinks in and oblivious to the tension. Margot was unimpressed, Sophie was nervous, and he was confused, aroused, and surprised all at the same time. Cecily was smiling prettily at no one, as she hung on to her husband's hand.

Sin grabbed Margot's hand first and bent over to kiss her gloved hand.

"It is such a pleasure to meet the woman who has made my friend so happy," he murmured politely.

She replied coolly, "How kind, I have heard much about you."

He ignored her emphasis and turned his attentions to Sophie. Everything and everyone else faded away as he grabbed her hand; the white satin glove provided little barrier to the heat that erupted at this contact. He brought her hand up to his lips but flipped it and placed a hot kiss to her pulse before he lifted his gaze to her jade eyes.

"It is a pleasure to meet you, your grace, I am Sinclair Montgomery."

Chapter Five

Sin *indeed*, Sophie gasped inwardly as she tried to refrain from fanning herself. The 'clair' had dropped off as soon as she met his gaze. This man could easily personify one of the seven deadly sins as lust erupted in her body. She had told the universe she wanted passion and now providence was tempting her with a simple kiss on the hand. Margot's derisive snort brought her out of her cascading thoughts and she quickly let go of Sin's hand. The twinkle of mirth in his dark eyes and his lazy smile told her he had not missed a second of her reaction.

"Ah, ladylike as always, dear wife," Daniel told Margot jovially with a kiss to her forehead.

"Well, if *Sin* does not mind, I think I shall stick with calling him *Sinclair* " Margot retorted as she linked arms with Sophie.

"You can call me anything you wish, beloved of my oldest friend. We will become fast friends yet." Sin winked at Margot and she failed to stop her blush at the charming but roguish gesture. Frustrated at the winking Sin and the guffawing Daniel, Margot hit the latter with her reticule.

"Lord help us to deal with men that are boys and fools," she proclaimed as she tugged Sophie away and gestured for Cecily to follow.

Sophie was still too stunned by her encounter with Sin to speak. She could not stop herself from casting a backward glance and saw his eyes were still on her. The distance made her braver and she gave him what she hoped was a coy smile. Her inner critic told her to stay away from Sin, but her inner heroine was telling her to indulge in one of the seven cardinal vices – and sin.

Sophie sipped at her rata"a as Margot raged to Cecily and some of the other women about the follies of rakes in the ton and how they should be made to live abroad during the season. "But Margot, was your husband not once a rake himself?" asked a tall brunette, whose name Sophie could not recall. The question held no sign of malice, just curiosity, but Margot's mouth dropped open in horror.

"Never! My Daniel may have had a few dalliances, but never did he do so with a lady, and he courted me with all the respect and chivalry one could want in a beau." Her chin jutted down at a stubborn angle. Sophie bit her lip to stop herself from laughing. A fiery Margot was always entertaining and would admit to her hot temper once cooler heads prevailed, but something about Sin really riled her up. Sophie also had the privilege, as Margot's best friend, of knowing about the roguishly stolen kisses and caresses she had shared with Daniel before they wed. They had giggled about them for hours on end with Sophie asking her to repeat every detail. She was two years older than Margot but had always taken the role of the younger sister in their friendship. Margot was always her staunch supporter.

Now, a change in topic was clearly needed, so Sophie asked Margot about the first opera they were planning to see. This proved a worthy distraction, as the women began to gossip all at once about who was playing what role and who had which seats. Satisfied that the group's attention was now completely focused on a topic that would go from strength to strength as far as gossip was concerned, she leaned over to Cecily.

"Cecily, I know you have an event planned for viewing it, but would it be an imposition for me to see the Botticelli? I hope you do not think me too forward for asking," she said in a soft whisper so no one else would hear.

Margot had confided this titbit in her, and Sophie had asked if it would be too forward to ask for a glance tonight. Sophie loved art, and knowing there was a famed artwork in the vicinity was too much to bear.

Cecily, endearing as always, smiled and nodded as she brought a finger to her lips and stood up. Giddy with excitement, Sophie stood with her, and splashed a little bit of ratafia on her dress.

"Oh, good idea, a guise!" Cecily applauded her quietly before turning loudly to the group.

"Sophie has soiled her dress. We must go and clean it up," Cecily announced.

Not my intention to highlight my clumsiness, but a small price to pay in the bigger scheme of things, Sophie thought as the women glanced sideways at her before turning back to their conversation. She knew James wanted to keep the painting veiled for a special event, but she would not be able to sleep tonight if she didn't get a chance to see it. She followed Cecily down a long hallway and into a library. In the middle of the room stood an easel, its contents draped. A servant had followed them in, and Cecily requested they light all the candles in the room.

"I will leave you to your admiration, Sophie. I have seen it so many times now it has quite lost its lustre. Come back the way we came and find me, and I will send for the candles to be snuffed." Sophie was astounded by Cecily's simple and pleasant attitude towards such a marvellous wonder. She stopped trying to understand the other woman and rushed to the easel. Gently, she pulled the sheet down inch by inch as she took a deep breath to contain her excitement. As the plain covering fell away, *The Birth of Venus* erupted in front of her eyes in a dizzying array of vibrant colours and textured strokes of creativity. Despite there being four figures in the painting, her eyes were automatically drawn to Venus herself. She held her fingertips as close as possible to the artwork without actually touching it and marvelled at her captured expression. Venus, in her mind, seemed unperturbed by what surrounded her as she rose from the clam shell in her nude glory. She looked resigned but beautiful, regal but without haughtiness. Sophie's eyes took in the ginger waves and soft white curves so like her own. She knew she boasted a more voluptuous figure, like those found in ancient stone carvings. They always filled her with confidence when she admired their beauty.

"Beauty. Such a work of beauty," she murmured as her eyes roved over the rest of the painting and noted the intricate details captured in this mythic event.

"A work of beauty indeed," said a husky voice from behind her.

Chapter Six

S in had spied Sophie walking o! with Cecily and muttered, "Wonder where they are off to."

Daniel readily answered, "Sophie must have asked to see the Botticelli that James is keeping quiet for the time being."

A Botticelli? James must have paid a dear price to have this painting on loan for the season. Sin himself was an admirer of Botticelli's captured beauty and grace that was both playful and sensual. He also did not want Sophie out of his sight. He was still seething at the lascivious looks slyly made in her direction. It occurred to him something was different about her in comparison to the other women. And then it hit him— her dress! It did not hang from her bust but instead gathered at her waist, accentuating her luscious curves.

"Which piece?" he asked curiously. "I must see it."

"Well James has a plan for its showing, but it appears that you, like Sophie, cannot be made to wait. I believe he has *The Birth of Venus* in his library, if you remember your way around here. And I will let him know. He will be irked by your impetuousness but unsurprised," Daniel said with a laugh and a shake of his head.

"I owe you one," Sin said and clapped him on the shoulder. "Another one, you mean?" Daniel called out after him.

If only Daniel's wife was as eager as Daniel to help him get close to Sophie. *If there is one thing I am good at, it is bringing a woman around to my way of thinking,* he thought, though he doubted that would work on Margot. *Interesting. I have never gone out of my way to befriend a woman. It makes sense that Daniel would marry a spirited one that would be at complete odds with me.* She was well matched to Daniel's even-tempered disposition.

Sin took the twists and turns to the library and avoided bumping into any guests. The door was open, so he stepped into the room without making a noise and stood for a few moments watching Sophie. He could only see her from the back but he could tell she was engrossed in her exploration of the famed painting. Her body language was tense in concentration, and he could see her hands hovering over the art, as if she wanted to touch it but knew she shouldn't. The self-restraint she demonstrated was more then he would be able to muster if those hands were his and she was the painting.

"Beauty. Such a work of beauty," she murmured, her tone filled with awe, and the genuine emotion he heard warmed him. It was not lost on him that his Goddess now stood in front of Venus, the Roman goddess of love, in all her splendid glory. Their gingered hair was a perfect match, and he imagined the same smooth alabaster curves underneath her dress as he felt himself grow hard. This Goddess was wreaking havoc on all his senses, and he needed to regain some control.

When Sin spoke, he was gratified by her startled jump as he watched a myriad of expressions cross her flushed face.

Annoyed? Because he interrupted her musings? He liked

her spirit. Embarrassed? At being caught almost nose to canvas? Her blush was endearing.

Flustered? At realising they were now alone and unchaperoned here in the library? He felt flustered himself.

"I beg your pardon. I thought I was alone," she said. Her eyes were downcast demurely, but he could hear the challenge in her tone.

"It seems that I was also too impatient to await the great unveiling. I had to see this masterpiece for myself."

She stepped aside to allow him a clearer view and he took the invitation to walk towards her. They stood side by side and the light !oral scent of honeysuckle and cinnamon teased his senses. It was a heady, delicious aroma.

"Well, what do you think, Sinclair?" she asked him eagerly.

He bit back a smile at her use of his first name and thought about his response. It was clear she also enjoyed the arts, so he paused his attempts at flirtation. "Many artists have tried to capture the famed scene, but I truly believe Botticelli does it best. Anyone can paint a shell and a body but it is her expression, the way he has captured the juxtaposition of modesty and haughtiness, that takes a true talent."

To his surprise, his genuine and thought-out answer had more of an impact then he imagined his flirting would have had, as he watched her doe eyes widen with pleasure.

"You know your art, Sin. You can interpret it beyond the surface. How unexpected," Sophie told him in her husky voice. It made him feel almost shy, to elicit this reaction by being simply himself and not falling back on the charm that had become so second nature.

"Well, yes. I have just returned from travelling abroad where I saw many famed works, sights, and museums. There is a world beyond our dreary, rainy London."

"How lucky you are! My longest travel from London was to Bath. And yes, we do have historical sites here at home but travelling abroad away must be like travelling to a different realm indeed," she said wistfully.

Suddenly, Sin wanted to know her more deeply. Not just to dance this dance till they found themselves in a pleasurable tryst. No. There was something about her. Something inside Sophie was searching for the zest in life, but he did not think she knew what it was. He held her gaze intently, and she blushed a little but did not look away.

"While ordinarily I would agree with you, standing here between this famed piece of art and you, a beautiful Goddess personified, is the first time I have seen something so appealing in London."

His head slowly descended and her fluttering eyelashes were all the signal he needed to press his lips to hers. Just as he felt their breath mingle, the moment was broken by a loud snort.

"How unoriginal!" said a glaring Margot from the doorway, hands on her hips. An apologetic Daniel shrugged behind her.

Sin sighed and gave a contrite bow in Margot's direction. "I can assure you I meant every word, but I would agree this is most improper. Please accept my apologies, both of you," he said, gesturing to Margot and Sophie.

"All is forgiven, Sinclair," Sophie said with sincerity. He turned, again noting the use of his first name, and her pale jade eyes now twinkled with mischief. It was evident his kiss would not have been a source of discontent for Sophie. *Oh Sophie, Goddess and saucy temptress. You will be mine.*

$$Chapter\ Seven$$

It was a beautiful day, yellow rays beamed through the fluffy clouds scattered across the blue sky. Margot had suggested they take tea outside and let her boys run around. And run around they did, as Sophie watched them zig and zag on their tiny toddler legs. They finally exhausted themselves and were napping on a blanket, which allowed Sophie and Margot to call for a fresh pot of tea they could drink before it got cold.

"No wonder you are in such a good shape," Sophie whispered, not wanting to wake them.

"You don't have to whisper, just not too loud, Soph," Margot said, one eye on her sleeping cherubs. "They do keep me trim, but I promised I would be a hands-on mother, unlike our own."

Sophie nodded with appreciation. Their mothers were friends, and both had parenting styles where children were not to be seen or heard. Thankfully, their nannies had become close friends as well, which allowed the girls much time spent together. Margot's mother was a tad warmer than her own and had at least allowed Margot to have a season. Sophie's parents did not want the fanfare and fuss that had come along with it.

And her mother never failed to remind her she would never be an incomparable. The giddiness of the stolen almost-kiss last night left Sophie wondering what she had missed out on by not having a season. Living vicariously through Margot had been exciting but to feel that reckless feeling herself had been exhilarating. Not that it was so scandalous, she was a widow after all. Most widows enjoyed a little more freedom, depending on how much you cared for gossip and standing.

Still, Sophie knew her parents would be horrified if she publicly shamed them by kissing a rake and allowing herself to be compromised.

Margot was watching her, waiting for her to bring up Sin. Sinclair. They had been distracted by the children but her grace period was now gone, and Margot was about to burst as she wriggled on the seat.

"I like him, Margot. I know you have taken an instant disliking to him and I am sure you have your reasons, but I am not an innocent virgin you need to protect. I am a mature widow." Sophie felt silly saying the last part out loud, and as soon as she locked eyes with Margot they burst out laughing before reminding each other to hush. Thankfully, the boys slept on.

"Soph, calling yourself a mature widow makes you sound our mothers' age. Though I know what you mean. I want you to enjoy yourself, but I do not want to see you hurt. And yes, I do have my reasons to dislike Sinclair Montgomery," Margot confirmed in a haughty tone.

"And those reasons are?" Sophie enquired, raising one eyebrow in curiosity.

"Reason one. You have only known one man, your husband, who was a dreadful bore. I am afraid going straight from that to a reprobate will leave you well out of your depth.

I am all for you finding a passionate dalliance, or something more like the marriage Daniel and I share. Sinclair is not a man for that, which leads me into reason two. His return means Daniel will spend time with him, and I do not want Sinclair leading Daniel back to his rakehell days which you know I whipped out of him."

"I sincerely doubt Daniel would ever step a toe over the line to cause you ire. But you are right about Sinclair. He is not in my league and I cannot compare to the beautiful, svelte women within the ton."

"Oh Soph, don't be dicked in the nob!"

The phrase took Sophie by such surprise she spilt her tea. Twice within two days she had spilt her drink upon herself. Margot handed her a napkin and composed herself while Sophie dabbed at the wet spot.

"Sorry for my outburst, Soph. But what you just said is not what I said in the slightest. And how can you think I would say such a thing? You, Sophie, are worth a thousand Sinclairs. And you, my dear Sophie, must stop comparing your own undeniable beauty to society's ideal of the moment. It was not the thin, fair-haired women Sinclair could not keep his eyes off. It was you. Ginger-haired and curvy in all the best places! All I did mean was that your heart needs protecting. I do not see him as a man to settle down anytime soon."

Sophie went over to Margot and gave her a warm embrace. "You are always my champion, Margot; I should not have assumed anything otherwise. But what if all I want is to experience passion and exploration? Maybe for now, just a tryst, to find out what I do and do not like. Once I have this experience, I can look for someone more compatible."

Margot did not seem convinced but did not argue her point any further.

"I will support your choices, of course. And if he puts those rakish lovemaking skills to use and I get to hear all the decadent details—that would be wonderful. But if he does break your heart, trust me when I say that I will knee him in the bollocks."

They shook hands on the plan, something they had always referred to as a gentleman's agreement. Just when Sophie felt like she could sit back and serenely finish a cup of tea, one of the cherubs awoke.

"Bollocks," said Jasper, to Margot's horror. "If anyone asks, he heard that from Daniel."

Chapter Eight

S in did not know what was worse for the current state of his hangover: the sharp sound of a drape being drawn back or the rays of light that hit him smack in the face. The erotic dream about the ginger-haired nymph with luscious curves started to fade.

Sophie. Sweet, delectable Goddess.

"Sorry, My Lord. Your father asked that I wake you," the servant said.

"Do not apologise. I am surprised he is not here doing it himself. What time is it?"

"Well after midday. I am also to tell you that I am your new valet; my name is Jack."

Now his dream had faded, and reality was setting in. He needed a plan. A plan to get to know Sophie better before someone stole that chance away.

"Well, Jack. I am unaccustomed to a valet after years of being a lone traveller, but I guess those days are over now that I am back home. Time to behave like a proper gentleman, eh?" He grinned over at the young lad as he swung his legs over the side of the bed. Jack grinned back, now at ease.

"I have drawn a bath and will get your clothes ready if that suits? And there are kippers and eggs waitin' downstairs. Cook said that was your favourite meal after a big evening out?"

"Cook would be right, Jack. Now let's get me bathed and dressed so I can tuck in."

Sin inhaled the aroma as well-seasoned, oiled, and buttered kippers were placed before him. Not a fancy, elegant meal or anything he imagined was too complex to make, just a simple meal Cook always did magnificently. He grabbed a slice of buttered toast, stuffed three kippers in the middle, and folded it, taking a big bite that left him with half.

"You still eat the same way, Sinclair. Even as a young lad, you always ate with this gusto, piling your food together and taking huge bites." His father had evidently been watching him.

"Food is one of the great pleasures in life," he replied with his mouth still half full.

"Gluttony is one of the seven sins." His father's eyes twinkled as they fell into their old banter.

"Better gluttonous and lustful than greedy and sloth-like." Sin knew the first two sins could be easily associated with his person. He enjoyed his food, enjoyed his women, and they were two things he would never apologise for.

"How was your evening, Sinclair? Was it a smooth transition back into polite society?"

"It was a terrific evening. Spending an evening with Daniel and James was as if all these years had not passed."

"Except they are now married, and Daniel fulfills his viscountcy with great aplomb."

Ah, back for scarcely a day and the shrewd old man is already working his agenda. Duty. Marriage. Responsibility.

Ignoring the intended segue, he responded without acknowledging the comment, "James has a Botticelli on loan. Magnificent piece of artwork. I saw some truly astonishing pieces while I was abroad. I am thinking of acquiring a few, ones I really took a fancy too."

There would be the added benefit of enticing Sophie to admire the art while he admired her, he thought with satisfaction.

"A happy topic for you indeed. What piece of art are you thinking of to draw such a gratified smile to your face?"

"Trust me when I tell you, Father, you do not want to know." Sinclair grinned.

"That is very kind of you Sinclair, but you have yet to shock me even after you hit your third decade a few short months ago. Now you are home, I understand you intend to pick up certain things where you left o", but I will remind you of your Montgomery duties. I am afraid we have come full circle, son."

Sin heard the faint plea in his father's voice and was hit with a pang of guilt. Because he had left his father all alone, they had each mourned Andrew's death alone and, while Sin had gallivanted from country to country, his father had continued with the responsibilities that came with being a member of the peerage.

"I know, Father, and I am ready and willing to step into my role as heir."

Acknowledging it out loud helped a little to assuage his grief and guilt and allowed him to accept his role in life. Estate management, political obligation and influence. As a second son he would have had some responsibility, though much less than a first born, and he had always been satisfied with that.

Sin looked around the room. The navy wallpaper emblazoned with white roses. The familiar silverware he had used his whole life. The paintings of landscapes that decorated the walls, displaying various holdings of the marquisate. And of course, the Montgomery family crest with its armoured medieval knight and peregrine falcon in ode to their Norman ancestry. Being the first or second son had never mattered, he was a Montgomery and needed to live up to the name. Now he was responsible for ensuring their lineage continued. He needed a wife. Faces of the women from last night danced before him but they were all a blur, as none had truly captured his interest. The only face that stood out was Sophie's. Those pale jade green eyes and the smattering of faint ginger freckles on her pert nose. He needed to learn more about her. She was a widow, but no children? But she was still young. She looked to be a young twenty-something. He would consult Daniel.

Damn, but do I want to court her or bed her? He knew both were possible, but finding a wife meant going about it in the proper way. The jealous reaction she evoked in him made it clear he wanted her, but to what end? Sin shook his head in a bid to clear his mind. There was plenty of time for that, but now he should focus on his father.

"Sorry for the woolgathering, father."

"What is on your mind? A woman?" he asked knowingly. Sin could not hold back his grin. "Indeed, it is a woman.

And what a woman! Not a young debutante on the marriage mart, but a mature and intelligent lady. A dowager duchess."

"Not very attractive, I assume?" His father tried to suppress a laugh.

"She is the most delectable woman I have ever seen, but my admiration is more than skin deep!"

"I am pleased to hear you thinking that way. A good woman is an asset in navigating life and all its follies."

"I have only met her the once, but I find myself besotted already. Is it lust or the start of something more?"

"Sounds to me as though this is the first time you have ever felt this way about a woman." His father's curious tone encouraged him to keep sharing his feelings.

"Never. She has stirred something primitive in me. And though I am still unsure of what I want from her, I do know I cannot allow any other man to have her."

His father's forehead crinkled in thought. "And she is a widow?"

"Yes, why?"

"Becoming a widow gives a woman a certain independence, especially one of her rank. She may not appreciate your jealousies. Your mother certainly did not."

"When did you ever act jealous?" Sin was thoroughly confused, recalling how happy his parents were. His father must have noticed his consternation, as he began to laugh.

"Before we were parents, we were a young, wedded couple. And before that, I courted her for months. You know how beautiful your mother was. When she debuted, every unwed man wanted to court her, and I was insanely jealous. It drove her crazy. She interpreted my jealousy as mistrust. The point I am trying to make is that when you find the right woman, no matter how other men lust after her, jealousy is a useless emotion if she has chosen you and only you."

This was a very wise lesson from his father. And Sophie did exude an independent nature, one he would have to be careful not to curb since that was part of her appeal.

"How insightful you are, old man," Sin exclaimed as he stood up and patted his father on the back.

"Don't you worry, there is plenty more wisdom to come. When will I learn her name?"

"Soon, Father, soon. I do not want to bring bad luck on myself until I find out more."

"I will await an update with bated breath. Is there anything else on your mind, son? You know you can share anything with me."

Sin hated the vulnerability he would show by voicing his deep-seated doubts out loud but he knew it was now or never.

"I worry I may not have it in me to be the man Andrew was."

"You won't be because you will be the man you are. I have two sons I am proud of. I never expected to outlive either of you, Sinclair. But I always knew I sired two good men. The only I regret I have is that your brother is no longer with us, not that you are not him."

"Thank you for that, father. Your faith in me gives me confidence that when I am faced with a challenge, I will make the right decision. Tell me what is to be done and it will be done."

The look of pride on his father's face humbled him and he knew stepping into this new version of himself would not be as daunting as it had seemed.

"The first lesson I will impart to you is the importance of taking care of our tenants. Come, let us go into the study."

Chapter Nine

A week had passed since Sophie had met Sinclair Montgomery and she had heard nought. Seen nought. Daniel had mentioned that he was touring his estates, but Sophie could not help but feel slightly rejected. And foolish. Had she imagined that spark of attraction, the desire that had sprung so naturally between them? In retrospect, she realised that was quite possible since she was a novice in these matters. Margot kept telling her to stop looking so blue-devilled—her state of melancholy apparent— and that he had never been worth the time to begin with, as she pointed out other men Sophie might be interested in. And there was no shortage of men. She danced, she made small talk, she agreed to let them call on her, but not a single one lit the spark that Sinclair had.

Sin.

She could say with certainty that he inspired the sin of lust and perhaps the sin of greed, as she could not imagine that a short period of time with him would be enough to satiate her burgeoning desire.

Sophie was also intrigued by his interest in art. What

wonders had he seen on his travels? Did he have any to call his own? She had been toying with the idea of collecting pieces herself. She loved the simple, exquisite beauty of the Ming Dynasty porcelain and wanted one of her own. Either a bowl or vase, and she would like it in a jade colour.

This is how she found herself alone in the carriage on her way to a well-known antiquities store: more well-known for what they could find rather than what they already had in stock. Daniel had secured her an appointment with Mr Welles, who only took referrals from members of the peerage. This was her first time out of the home on her own in weeks, and as much as she loved the company of Margot and her family, it was a pleasant change of pace to be alone with her thoughts in the carriage. She wore one of her new day dresses, a Carmelite brown, accented with a white trim around the bust, waist, and hands that flattered her curves. Sophie had chosen all white accessories; her parasol, hat, gloves, and even shoes were all shades of white to cream. She had felt vain as she admired her ensemble when she caught sight of herself in the mirror before she left.

But as she pondered her inner critic's accusation of vanity she realised that the feeling was misidentified. Her self- admiration was actually pride. She looked and felt every inch the independent and competent widow, and her inner self- confidence was something she had to embrace, not discourage. The carriage came to a halt, and within moments the driver assisted her down and escorted her to the door of a nondescript storefront.

The curtain in the single window was closed, however the sign on the door said 'Open—please use the knocker'. She looked up to confirm that she was at the right place and saw a sign that said 'Welles & Welles.' She looked back down to the brass lion's head knocker and gave it a few sharp taps. She was about to do it again when a balding, bespectacled man opened the door.

"Ah, my 9:30. Come in, Your Grace," he said with a flourish of welcome.

Sophie crossed the threshold and gasped. Every possible surface was covered with more things than she could count. Furniture, books, statuettes, clocks, and lamps. She felt a shiver run down her spine when she spied the eerie taxidermy that stared back at her as she gazed around the room. It would take months to catalogue the contents of this room.

"A usual first impression, madam. My objects of collection and curiosities never fail to stun," he informed her cheerily.

Sophie smiled at the odd fellow. She liked him.

"It is certainly an impressive inventory you have, Mr Welles; you clearly have a skill in acquisition."

"Thank you, madam. Follow me into my office so we can sit and discuss what it is you want me to find."

The office was just as full, but mainly of books and papers. And Sophie spied a black cat sleeping on one of the chairs—a live one. Mr Welles situated them on either side of a desk in the middle of the room and poured some tea from a cast iron teapot, aged but in impeccable condition.

He must have seen her admiring it. "An early Japanese sixth century teapot; the cast iron retains the flavour of tea wonderfully. But if I am correct, we are to speak of another Orient, the Ming Dynasty of China?"

"That is true, but I may be adding a teapot to my list!"

"That can be easily done. Now tell me more of this object you seek." His posture was now alert and focused as he leant forward, spectacles perched on the end of his nose.

"Well, I am certain it is no surprise that what I am after is a porcelain bowl. Ideally, one in green with a floral pattern. I believe a lotus flower?"

Mr Welles nodded as she spoke, a smile widening across his round face.

"How extraordinary! This is the second request within the week for this same object," he told her excitedly as he pushed his spectacles up the bridge of his nose. "Now, asking for a Ming bowl is quite ordinary, but with the same unusual colour and pattern? How very curious."

Sophie was taken aback. In all the scenarios she had envisioned, having it slip between her fingers to someone else's had not occurred to her.

"Who is this?" she asked him abruptly, forgetting her manners.

"My apologies, but I cannot divulge my clientele. My reputation is built on being discreet," he replied, slightly aghast.

"No. I am sorry, Mr Welles. I should not have been so forward. You will still keep me apprised of any success?"

"Of course. I may find more than one and if not, we could arrange a silent auction."

"Thank you for your time, Mr Welles. I look forward to hearing from you soon."

Sophie managed a gracious smile as she hid her disappointment. All there was to do was wait. Wait for word from Mr Welles. Just like the word she was waiting to hear from Sinclair Montgomery.

Chapter Ten

Sin silently willed the horse-drawn carriage to go faster. The sound of their hoofbeats hitting the ground seemed to compound every second. It was Wednesday, and he wanted to make it home in time to attend Almack's. He was certain Sophie would be in attendance; the first Almack's affair of the season always drew in the crème de la crème. Daniel and Margot would have been invited, and Sophie would surely accompany them. Fidgeting, he tapped the joint of his index finger against the glass window and let out a sigh.

"Son, you have been on edge ever since we got in the carriage. What concerns you?" his father asked in a tone that was as amused as it was annoyed.

"I'm fine, just eager to get back to London. I want to attend Almack's at a reasonable hour, is all."

"Since when do you care for proper appearances?" His father's eyebrows lifted in surprise.

Sin could not help the little smile that spread across his face at his father's bemused reaction. He had been seeing those lifted brows quite a bit during their time spent together. His father clearly had not expected Sin to remember as much as he did about the management of their holdings. Sin took pride in his father's praise at the natural way of he engaged with everyone they encountered. Not stuffy but approachable. Sin explained that his years travelling as a common man among common men had taught him about living more simply and humbly. A lesson he would not have gained by continuing to live a pampered life that catered to his every whim.

"I want to make a good impression, father. Tonight's a!air is always a highlight of the season. You know that."

"Ah, I see. It is that mysterious woman," he said in a knowing voice.

"Indeed, it is, and I have been without the sight of her for so long. I hope I will be able to control myself."

"At least assure me that whatever you are up to will not result in scandalous gossip, will you?"

"I promise there will be no gossip, but I cannot promise I may not behave in a way that is improper."

"Just remember what I said. Do not let irrational thoughts cloud your judgement."

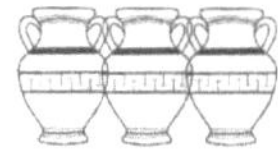

Sin arrived at Almack's as an early guest, showing the ticket and voucher that had been waiting for him at home. He was glad he had arrived early, as he wanted an unobstructed view of the entrance so he could see Sophie when she arrived. He felt a right fop as he tugged nervously at his pristine white cravat. He would never admit to anyone how utterly nervous and excited he felt as he anticipated the moment.

This must be how these daft chits feel every day on the marriage mart, he thought as he eyed the young women steadily arriving. They flocked together like geese as they eyed him hopefully and giggled behind their fans. Unbeknownst to them, they would be sorely disappointed come evening's end when he had not asked to sign anyone's dance cards. The mothers and chaperones of these women, however, were another story. He watched them eye him brazenly, their gazes calculating and scheming. *Must avoid eye contact*, he reminded himself repeatedly. He took a sip of the claret he was holding and tasted the hint of blackberry and thyme as he swirled the liquid around in his mouth. An oakish aftertaste came through, but it finished on a fruity note. It wasn't one of the most expensive vintages he had drunk, but it was better than rata!a and the other sickly-sweet refreshments.

A jolt ran through his body and instantly he knew Sophie was here. He looked up and saw her enter with Daniel and Margot, but they faded away as his vision narrowed down to only her. Her bewitching ginger strands were piled atop her head, little ringlets springing forth. Her gown, he noticed again, was different from the other women's. The waist sat lower and cinched her hourglass frame. His blood heated. He fought for calm as he studied the curvature of her body, lest he get an obvious erection in such polite company. Like last time, he saw an appreciative gleam in the eyes of the men she passed but he suppressed any jealousy. He heard Daniel call his name and turned to the sound of his voice. Daniel spoke to Margot and Sophie and gestured that they should join Sin. He saw Sophie's smile of pleasure and Margot's frown of displeasure and gave them both his most charming smile.

"Sin, you are back! How was the sojourn to the country-side?" Daniel welcomed him with a warm smile and handshake.

"It was enlightening, to say the least! I am glad to be back amongst friends," Sin replied to him. He smiled at Margot and lifted her hand for a kiss. Too eager to wait for a response, he turned to Sophie and grabbed one of her hands with both of his as he pulled it to his mouth. Using his hands to obscure his actions, he turned her hand over and kissed the beating pulse at her wrist.

"How have you fared since I last had the pleasure of seeing you, Sophie?" he asked, still holding onto her hands. Her beautiful eyes had widened, and her pink pout had formed an O shape, shocked at his brazen kiss. She blinked a few times and shook her head, composing herself as she snatched her hand away.

"I have been very well; very, very well."

The blood in Sin's veins thrummed at the knowledge that he was having this impact on her senses. Her tone was forced, breathless, and harried. The repetition spoke to her nerves, and, in turn, her nervous energy excited him. It did not matter who else looked at her in want, Sophie reciprocated his desire.

Within seconds, others had joined their circle and there was chatter from every angle, which made it hard to snare a moment of Sophie's direct attention. He eyed her side profile, the delicate sweep of her nose with a sprinkle of freckles and the soft arch in her eyebrow, a few shades darker than her hair. Still ginger but a darker colour, almost brown if she was at a distance. He loved her ginger hair and it conjured Venus in his mind again. If he was the artist depicting the birth of Venus, he would paint Sophie. She would be in all her nude glory, draped over an ornate chaise. Her full breasts would peek between her ginger hair, which would be brushed long over the front of her shoulders. Attendants would serve her every need, feeding her grapes and champagne. Sin himself had the distinct image of dripping something sweet like honey over the contours of those delicious curves, licking the sweet nectar from her soft skin with his tongue.

"—Sin, Sin?" Daniel was trying to draw his attention. "What is it?" he said, trying to gain control over his senses.

"The first dance is about to start. I am going to escort Margot," Daniel said with a pointed glance towards Sophie.

"Oh, right. Yes!" Sin said, turning to Sophie, "May I have your hand in a dance?".

"I would be delighted," Sophie said, her voice a little throaty, which matched the pleasure in her smile as she stepped in front of the sweep of his hand. Interpreting this as a positive sign, he took the opportunity and snuck a cheeky squeeze of her buttocks as she brushed by. Risky, but there were so many people about that no one would see. The flesh he grabbed was soft, plump, firm—a perfect peach. A peach he desperately wanted to sink his teeth into.

Chapter Eleven

I cannot believe he pinched my bottom!

Sophie's face flamed at the intimate gesture, but she could not deny the tingling warmth that spread between her thighs from this touch. The first dance did not help calm her passions since it was a waltz, which meant there was a certain closeness. Inhaling subtly, she breathed in his scent and quivered. She smelt wood, fresh pine, and a hint of vanilla. A masculine smell with a touch of sensuality. Their height difference meant her head just reached his shoulder and she could hear the thump of his heart. It was beating a little fast in her opinion.

Did I have the same effect on him?

She tilted her head upwards to watch his face and took a sharp breath when she found him already staring down at her with a slow, sexy smile showing off his perfect teeth. His skin had a golden glow that was evidence of time spent outdoors, which contrasted handsomely against his dark eyes. A lock of hair had tumbled onto his forehead and gave him an endearing look that contrasted with his raw masculinity.

"I like the way you feel in my arms, Sophie," he said in a low, seductive tone.

The lady in her should have been o!ended, but she reminded herself what it was she wanted. She wanted—no, needed—to feel passion. And all the blood pulsing in her body knew he could give her that. Attempting to be flirtatious, she adopted what she hoped was a coy smile rather than one that made her look like a fool.

"I admit, *Sin*, I am very much enjoying it as well. Your embrace is so strong and comforting. And all we are doing is waltzing."

She knew he caught her implication when his eyes darkened, black as sin, and his grip on her hand and waist tightened.

"I appreciate a woman who speaks her mind."

"Well, that is exactly what I am compared to many of the debutantes here. A woman. A widow."

"Indeed you are, which is something else I appreciate. I hope we can spend time together so we can enjoy our mutual interests, such as our passion for art and other things we will discover when we are alone."

Her worry that she was too brazen was overshadowed by the excitement she felt in playing the role of seductress. She genuinely felt safe in his presence and her impatience was brewing. There was a limit to how forward she could be, and she might need to be more creative with her hints.

"You are most welcome to call on me any time. Perhaps you have some art you can show me soon?" she suggested, keeping her tone airy.

"I am setting my own rooms up over the next few days, and you will be the first person I invite over." His tone held a darker edge now. It was sexy, commanding, and full of wicked promise. Sophie's knees buckled slightly and she felt a growing dampness between her legs. It was like he saw straight through her as he eyed her with a smug and knowing look. The dance was about to end, and he bent closer so she could feel his hot breath in her ear.

"Look how I have aroused you with just words and soft touches. Imagine what I will do to you once I have you alone, my Goddess."

Margot thrust a drink at Sophie.

"Here, have a glass of rata"a, Soph. You looked flushed."

"Thank you, Margot. It is so warm in here." Sophie fanned herself furiously as she relived the moments of that provocative dance. The dance itself had felt so natural, each step in rhythm like their bodies knew each other intimately, even though their minds had not yet made that same connection.

"Sophie, are you listening to me?" asked Margot in exasperation.

"Yes, sorry. What did you say?" She gave Margot her rapt attention.

"You are falling for him. One dance and look at you, you are about to melt into a puddle!"

"I am not! I was just enjoying the moment. He makes me feel desired in a way I have never felt before."

"I know, darling, and for that I am thrilled, you know that. I just don't want to see you hurt."

"Can I not live in these moments wholeheartedly, knowing it will only be moments? Having no expectations?"

"You can most certainly try, Soph, but matters of the heart are tricky. And good intentions and rationale will be no match for emotions if you fall for him. Look, let me have Daniel do some reconnaissance on Sinclair so we can ascertain what his intentions are."

Sophie shook her head at the suggestion. If she went from brazen widow to widow seeking commitment, it would dampen their flirtation and current understanding. It would be better to sin than never to have Sin at all. And she wanted him to ravish her!

"No, you do not need to do that. I want to let things play out on their own. Promise you will not say anything to Daniel."

"I promise, I promise," Margot said with a sigh. "I just hope you know what you are doing."

Daniel and Sin joined them moments later. Sin expressed his apologies, he needed to leave. Sophie could not help but feel disappointed as she had hoped for another dance but saw Margot eyeing her so she masked her expression. Sin kissed her hand in farewell—the same way he had greeted her—and she felt the hot kiss on her wrist like a brand.

"I will call on you soon, Sophie. Be ready for me." He gave her one of those slow, sexy smiles and sauntered away.

Breathe, Sophie, breathe.

Chapter Twelve

A note arrived for Sophie within a few days, as Sin had promised, and she pictured the words in her mind as she looked out the carriage window.

S,

My carriage will call for you at 12 o'clock on Tuesday, the 15th. Anticipation makes for an intoxicating aphrodisiac.

Yours, S

She unfurled her fan and beat it furiously in an attempt to cool her rising temperature. There was no mistaking his meaning – she was en route to meet him for a tryst! She had prepared herself very carefully today, soaking in scented bath water until she was certain the soft notes of roses and lilies had permeated her skin. All of her underthings were brand new and had accents of soft silk and delicate lace. She felt decadent and scandalous and her inner critic and inner heroine battled, alternately tipping the scales between confidence and embarrassment. Confidence was winning, as she knew Sin desired her. Her petticoat and shift accentuated her hourglass shape, her stays cinched at the waist and gave her bust a slight lift. She had forgone drawers as they were unflattering and, if she was correct in what Sin had planned, most likely a waste of time. Similarly, she steered away from anything too complicated with her hair and had piled it on her head with Grecian clips. Sophie had chosen a white day dress and a beige spencer that matched her gloves and shoes, as there was a chill in the air. She felt stylish in an understated way, at least with her outer clothing.

It appeared they were headed to The Albany in Piccadilly – notorious bachelor quarters and known for its discretion. It was unlikely she would bump into anyone she knew, but to err on the side of caution she would use her parasol and fan for concealment. The assignation was almost upon her and butterflies began a crazed waltz in the pit of her belly. She was no virgin but neither was she experienced in the ways of pleasure. Her late husband had established the monotony of her wifely duties at the outset of their marriage. She knew there was something missing but the lack of intimacy and desire on both their parts had kept it perfunctory. She knew he had a mistress, as discreet as he was, but she was never jealous, just envious that she had no passionate outlet of her own.

The carriage slowed down as she arrived at her destination, and she sat up straight and inhaled a deep breath.

Sin paced the foyer, only stopping to spy at the window to see if Sophie had arrived. He wanted to take her upstairs, strip her naked and be inside of her. He knew he had to cool his ardour;

she was still a lady. But the thought of her heated his blood like no woman ever had. And he did not want her just for today. The more he had considered a future with her over the last few days, the more settled on the idea he became. He had conducted some reconnaissance in this time and learned her marriage was arranged and had never blossomed into more. The man had kept a mistress, likely resulting in many lonely nights for Sophie. Which Sin found utterly ridiculous— Sophie was a Goddess!

His head snapped around to look out the window as he heard the sound of wheels on gravel. There she was. Sunlight bounced o" the vibrant ginger hair that peeked out from underneath her hat as the driver escorted her out of the carriage. Sin wanted to race outside and meet her but for propriety's sake he restrained himself and waited till she stepped inside. Thankfully, he had thought ahead and paid the doorman to make himself scarce.

"Sophie, what a vision you are," he said as he grabbed her hand to plant a firm kiss.

"Good day, Sinclair." Her voice was honied as she beamed brightly in greeting.

"Let's get you upstairs. I have a surprise for you."

"Oh how intriguing" She took his hand without hesitation as he guided her to his rooms. Their light stream of chatter came naturally, and if it wasn't for the furious pounding of his heart he would have felt completely at ease.

"Can I offer you any refreshment?" Sin enquired.

"No, I am fine, thank you, just curious about my surprise." Her cheeks held the tinge of a blush.

"A lady with a singular focus." He was unable to help giving her a wink. "My kind of lady.

"I have acquired a piece of history that I am confident you will appreciate," he informed her as he walked over to a covered object on the table.

"It looks like vase or pot of some kind. Is it Grecian?" she asked in a breathy voice, her excitement evident.

"What instincts you have, Sophie! It is Grecian from the Attica region: a volute krater, a bowl used for mixing wine and water." He revealed the precious artefact with a flourish as he pulled o" the covering.

The ancient artefact was still in wonderful condition, considering it had been dated between 490 and 460 BC. It was a unique piece because the painted artwork was con#ned to the top of the pot and handles, while the rest of the body was painted black except for some decoration around the bottom.

"How fascinating," she whispered as she eyed the pot closely. "The paintwork is so vivid, and the figures are even labelled. I can see Achilles and Hector battling one another while Athena and Apollo observe. This is obviously a depiction of a scene from the Trojan War."

Sin was impressed by the insight and knowledge she had gathered in a few short moments as she walked around the pot absorbing every intricate detail.

"A lover of the arts and histories," he murmured.

"You cannot love one without the other," she said with a small shrug, eyes still on the pot. "Where do you plan on keeping it?"

"I will have it moved to my townhouse and perhaps then to my country estate. You can visit it whenever you like." He was unable to resist the opening. This made her turn and lock her eyes with his.

"Keep acquiring pieces like this, and I will be unable to resist, Sin." There was a low purr in her voice as she said his name.

"That is my plan indeed, to lower your resistance," he said as he stepped towards her. They were now so close he could feel her breasts slightly heaving against his chest as he looked down into her jade eyes.

"You have no idea, Sophie, how I have longed to be so close we can share each breath and feel our bodies pulse against each other. You bewitched me from the moment I saw you, ginger- haired and buxom like you had just arisen from a shell in the ocean."

Her breath quickened as his words washed over her and her gaze lowered to his mouth. The tip of her pink tongue poked out and she moistened her lips in what he hoped was anticipation. That was all the invitation he needed to crush his lips to hers with no finesse, just a frenzied need to satiate himself with her intoxicating ambrosia.

Chapter Thirteen

Sophie had had no idea passion like this existed before Sin plundered her mouth with such sensual ferocity. The feeling of his tongue in her mouth was a pleasant surprise that made her moan against his lips. She clung to his waist lest her knees buckle, and she revelled in the strong grip he had on her. One hand held her firmly at the nape of her neck and the other had roughly pulled out her hair clips and was now entangled in her tresses. It did not take her long to find her rhythm as she returned his kisses. Hers were just as heated and as fierce and the gratification of his groans only spurred on her arousal.

"Sophie, I have a confession to make." He broke o" the kiss and left her panting. Sin's dark eyes bore into her own and she tried to hold his gaze, terriffed he was about to ruin the moment.

"Tell me what it is. Unburden yourself." Her voice was a mere whisper.

"I have this fantasy of you, playing over in my mind without any relief. Of you naked upon a chaise like the one behind you. Draped in only the luscious femininity currently hidden beneath all that cloth."

"So I please you, Sin?" Her inner critic appeared, looking for validation.

"Sophie, you please me more than any woman ever has. I never thought I had a weakness, till I met you. You are the definition of woman." He traced her curves, caressed the roundness of her belly, and squeezed the flesh of her buttocks "You are the embodiment of perfection."

She didn't answer him but stood up and turned around so he faced her back. This was the moment to embrace herself and own her desires. She began to pull at the ties at the front and that was all the invitation he needed to start undoing the dress at the back. Her dress and underclothes came off in quick succession till she was nude, all but for her stockings and slippers. His touch was feather soft as his fingertips grazed her skin gently, tracing a line or a fold, and even though she could not see his face she could tell from his quickened breath that he was excited.

He must have dropped to his knees, because she felt him tug at her slippers. He traced his fingers up her legs to where her stockings sat and teased her aching mound by stroking the moistened flesh. Sophie felt him press a kiss to the top of her buttocks before he rolled down her stockings on each leg.

She was now completely nude, vulnerable, and standing there in all her womanly glory. She didn't wait for instructions and turned to face him; his head was now level with the centre of her core. Sin let out a pained groan and a whispered *fuck*. The next moment she gasped her own oath as his mouth covered her moistened need. Sophie clutched his head like it was an anchor as he devoured her with his tongue. His confident and learned strokes confirmed he was no novice when it came to giving a woman pleasure. His fingers joined his exquisite mouth, and she lost all her senses as she fell back into the chaise with her legs flung apart. Her behaviour was the picture of a pure wanton, but she did not care. All that mattered was this race, the race between his lips, tongue, and fingers to see which would undo her first. She fought for breath as waves of ecstasy started to roll through her body.

"Sin, oh my goodness. Sin, my god!" Sophie managed to sputter out as magnificent sensations she had never known existed coursed through her and peaked.

"That's a good girl, Sophie. Come for me. Come all over me, you are mine," he growled.

The idea that she was his sent her over the edge, and her body reverberated with spasms so exquisitely pleasurable it almost seemed magical. As the tremors subsided, she was shaky, sweaty, and replete. She looked down at Sin, his head still between her legs, as he gave her a lazy grin.

"And that wasn't even the entirety of what I had wanted to confess."

"Truly, I don't how my body could withstand more of that, it was so wickedly decadent." Her body had never been so languid as she arched her back to stretch.

He stood, unfairly still clothed, and went over to a picnic basket. He gestured for her to sit on the chaise.

"Since I laid eyes upon you, I've had this fantasy that I cannot shake. You are naked on a chaise, being fed grapes, drinking champagne, and drizzled with honey like a goddess in an ancient painting. Except I am the only one in the painting with you, worshipping you, feeding you grapes." He deftly pulling a grape from the bunch in the basket and popped it into her mouth. "Pouring your champagne." With "ute and bottle in hand, he poured her a glass. She accepted the drink, needing something cool to slake her thirst.

"And honey that I would lick off your luscious body."

Sin drizzled honey over her breasts which now heaved in anticipation. The sticky golden syrup clung to her soft white skin as it formed a trail from one rosy hard nipple to the other. Sophie tried to remain calm and aloof, as sexy and sultry as she imagined a temptress might be, but she knew she was failing miserably as her body shook with eagerness and desire. Sin must have sensed that she was feeling vulnerable and began to undress so they would be on common ground. Now that he was nude before her, all she could think of were ways to get on top of him, be under him, or any other position they could join as one. She lowered her eyes to the hardened proof of his desire and licked her suddenly dry lips. It was a piece of art—long, smooth, and thick—and she needed it to fill every inch of her core.

Sin sat on the chaise and popped a grape in her mouth, then kissed her with his own mouth full of champagne. The sweet grape and bubbly champagne fizzled naughtily in her mouth as he nibbled on her lower lip. Sin pulled Sophie closer to him on the chaise and began to lick the honey from her hardened nipples. She moaned as he sucked the rosy peaks almost roughly which aroused her more as she moved her hands to grip his head.

"Ah Sin, that feels so *sinfully* delicious," she crooned, wanting him to know how much she was enjoying his touch.

"You taste wickedly delicious, Sophie, sweeter than any nectar the gods would indulge in." The slight growl in his voice sent another jolt of lust straight to her core as she fell back on the chaise. *The pleasure was too much!*

Sin continued to follow the trail of honey down her body with his tongue. Each erotic stroke of his tongue had her panting and mewling. Finally, he sat back with a proud and satis!ed smile on his face as his dark eyes twinkled.

"You have been thoroughly licked clean, Sophie," he told her as he leant back on the chaise with legs open and crooked his finger for her to come closer. "Sit astride me. Be a good girl and ride me."

Never having experienced sex except on her back, she hesitated, not from fear but from embarrassment. The premise was straightforward, but what if she did it wrong? But his praise of her and demand she be a good girl became a desperate urge she must fulfil. She wanted to please him as he did her.

Sophie straddled Sin and positioned herself where they would join as one. Sin watched her with hooded eyes and a lazy grin as he guided her hand to his erection and encouraged her to touch it. It was rock hard, but the skin was soft as she rubbed it up and down. She enjoyed the feel of it pulsating in her hand. Pulling herself up, she guided it to her wet folds and rubbed the tip of his erection at her opening to ensure the position was right. The sensation elicited a moan from her, and Sin seemed to enjoy it just as much, as his breath turned ragged. Lowering herself slowly, she took him in inch by inch, marvelling at the exquisite sensation as he filled her. They were both panting and moaning as Sin clutched her waist, his head thrown back in ecstasy. She lowered herself the final inch and suddenly she was full, full of Sin.

Chapter Fourteen

Sin was in an unprecedented state of desire. This voluptuous Goddess astride him seemed to be too good to be true as her ample breasts jiggled tantalisingly in his face. Sin grabbed her buttocks as she started to ride him faster and found her rhythm. He urged her on with slaps to the fleshy cheeks.

"God, I love how I can grab on to your body, Sophie. You are so utterly delicious," he told her roughly between pants, as he dug his fingers into her soft flesh. He wanted to leave his mark on her. He wanted her to be all his. He could tell she was unaccustomed to lovemaking in this position, which pleased him immensely on a primal level. Knowing he was the first man to make her feel this way was an aphrodisiac on its own. *And I will be the last man,* he told himself fiercely as he pumped away. Sophie's jade gaze had transcended pure passion and was now a vision of ecstasy as her climax began to build again.

"Come for me, Sophie. I want to feel you squeeze me as your body starts to unravel." She could only respond with a moan, too far gone in her rapture for words. Sin felt his own climax was near, and he tried to hold it back as he wanted Sophie to peak first. His legs were shaking with desire as he sought self-control. Just when he was about to explode, he felt Sophie's muscles tense around his cock, squeezing him as she cried out in orgasmic release. Her body fell against him as the waves crashed over her. He gripped her to him and roared as his own release shot deep inside her, claiming her as his. He fell against the chaise on his back, with Sophie still on top of him, and all he could hear was their uneven breathing as their bodies relaxed in the aftermath of their lovemaking. Sin placed kisses on her shoulders as he stroked her back with gentle care.

"Sin, never in my wildest fantasies had I imagined my body could feel that way," Sophie finally spoke, awed.

"I am no novice, Sophie, but even for me that was truly astounding. Maybe you really are a Goddess, Venus reincarnated."

Sophie giggled against his skin. "You flatter me too much, Sin."

"Yes, but it is all truth," he said with seriousness as he sat them back up. He stood to fetch them refreshment, as he knew they would both be thoroughly dehydrated after such intense lovemaking. Sitting back down, he handed her a glass of water.

"Sophie, you must know that for me this isn't some affair or meaningless tryst. I want to marry you." He was sure he could have made this sound more romantic, but he had no idea how. This type of conversation was foreign to him. He had tripped over lust and fallen into love, and he was unable to stop himself from letting her know.

Disappointment sank low in his belly when, instead of looking pleased, she frowned.

"I am flattered, Sin, but I am not looking to remarry at the moment. You must understand. I spent years married to a man I did not choose and never came to love. My whole life was dictated for me until I found myself widowed. I am not ready to lose my newfound identity."

Despite the hurt of rejection, Sin realised her feelings had more to do with her and the past than with him and the future.

"I would never take your identity away. Who you are in this moment is the Sophie I adore. The clever, art-loving, sexy Sophie."

"You are an heir to a marquessate and I am not sure I can even have children to pass your title on to. You have only recently returned from abroad; don't you want to see what options there are on the marriage mart? Younger and more polished debutantes, the diamonds and incomparables? I am the exact opposite of all that." She gestured towards her still naked and voluptuous figure.

"Sophie. The thought of tying myself to one of those simple waif-like chits does the exact opposite of making my cock hard. The future I see for myself is days spent with a full-bodied woman with fiery ginger hair and jade eyes that can talk art and history, and banter daily with her clever wit. And just because you did not come to be with child in your first marriage does not mean the problem lies with you."

Sin realised his conceit, as he had assumed his o"er of marriage to any woman would be met with a resounding yes. What a sobering moment. He rubbed his face in his hands.

"Sin, I do not mean to hurt you or sound unfeeling. Give me time? And perhaps you should also take some time to consider if this is what you want."

He could not be angry at her; this forthright logical honesty is what he admired about her.

"Of course. I do not plan on giving up; I know what I want. You. All I can do now is try to convince you to change your mind. Do you want to view the pot again?"

He knew she would need to leave soon and didn't want

their last moments after such a magnificent time spent together to end on anything but a high note.

"I would love to! Let me dress first." As she dressed, she looked around his quarters. They boasted a drawing room, bedroom, dressing room, bathroom, and study. The rooms all had tasteful and expensive furniture made of cherry, oak, and mahogany with a masculine "air and no "orals or feminine touches. It was a typical bachelor lodging.

"I do hope you move the pot to your townhouse in order to give visitors an opportunity to marvel at its beauty. I would not imagine you do much socialising in your rooms."

"Yes, the rooms are a necessity to keep some space from my father, but I spend most of my time with him or at White's since I still have many old friends to be reacquainted with. Perhaps you and I, along with Daniel and Margot, could take in an opera next week?" He did not want her to leave without having some certainty of when he would see her next.

"I believe Rossini's *Il barbiere di Siviglia* is playing at the King's Theatre. I would love to see it," she said giving him a warm smile. He could tell by the light in her eyes that she was happy he had already asked to see her again—this gave him hope.

"Consider my company to be all yours.".

Chapter Fifteen

argot thought it was a good idea to take the children for a picnic in Hyde Park while the weather was nice. Sophie now seriously questioned the idea, as the two boys wrestled each other every time Margot and Daniel let go of them. They were now trying with some success to convince the boys to take a nap.

"I think I would love to have a girl first," Sophie said out loud.

"Since when were you thinking of having children?" Margot asked.

Sophie had not regaled her with the entire truth of the events of her trip to Sin's, but had given a tamer version of their lovemaking. She had definitely not told Margot of his proposal. She would eventually, but for now she wanted her thoughts and decisions to be completely her own and not tainted by any other opinions.

"It was just a thought. I don't know if I would have the energy like you do, Margot, to keep up with your sweet boys," she said, looking at their perfect faces. They certainly looked like little angels even though they acted like little imps.

"Trust me, it just comes to you. I never actually feel the exhaustion until my head finally hits the pillow at night."

"Which is a shame, since it means I get no quality time with my wife," Daniel joined in, giving Margot a wink.

"How have you kept this spark and banter alive in your marriage?"

Daniel shrugged. "When it is the right person, your soulmate, it comes naturally."

"Are you thinking of marrying again, Soph?" asked Margot. She clearly sensed something was amiss. This was a perk of being best friends, but also a downfall. She could not hide anything for too long. Luckily, Daniel saved her from responding as he started to wave.

"Sin, Sin! We are over here," he called out.

Sophie's head snapped around so fast she felt a twinge of discomfort in her neck.

Margot noticed Sophie's wince. "Blazes! You just heard the man's name, and you almost broke your neck."

Sophie brushed her off and sat up as he approached. "Good day all," he greeted them happily. When his eyes landed on Sophie, he gave her a knowing smile and her toes curled.

"Glad we bumped into you, Sin. I was going to send word later, but I shall let you know now that we would love to go to the opera. Or we would love you to join us, as I have a box for the season with a terrific view." Daniel was oblivious to his wife's disapproving glare.

"Wonderful! I have not been to the West End since I returned home."

"Well, it was nice seeing you, Sinclair, but we really must get the boys home." Margot gestured to the stirring children.

"I understand," Sin said with a nod as he turned to Sophie. "Perhaps I can interest you in a walk around the park and then I can see you home?"

Sophie nodded, not looking back to Margot, who would be furious. Sin's cheeky smile told her all she needed to know.

The sun was quite bright, especially in the direction they were walking, so Sophie put her parasol to effective use. Sin did not seem to mind, walking as if he had eyes at the top of his head, his neck craned down and gaze fixed upon her.

"Have you thought about my offer?" he asked abruptly.

"I have, but it occurred to me that I have only seen you a handful of times. I barely know you."

"I challenge that for two reasons. Most spouses barely know each other before they wed, and I would say we know each other very intimately." His heated gaze sent a tingle of desire through her body.

"This is true, but perhaps for my next marriage I would prefer to know my husband, and not only in an intimate sense."

"Very well, what do you want to know, Sophie? I am an open book."

"Why did you leave England?"

A pained look appeared on his face at this question.

"Has Daniel not mentioned it to you?" His tone was casual, but there was still pain in his eyes.

"No, he has not divulged anything to me."

"My older brother passed away, suddenly and tragically in a horse-riding accident. I left because London held too many memories of him. I needed space and distance to grieve."

Sophie grabbed his hand and gave it a tight squeeze.

"I am so sorry for your loss. Thank you for sharing that with me."

"And I for yours. You lost your husband."

"I did, but it cannot be compared to your loss. In truth, I did not grieve him for long. He was a good man, but we were strangers."

"It is rude to speak ill of the dead, but the man was an idiot to not have seen the precious gem you are."

"Beauty is in the eye of the beholder, I suppose. So, tell me more. What is your favourite food?"

"Well, when I am nursing a sore head after a drink or two, kippers and eggs make me feel a treat. What is yours?"

"I am afraid I have a bit of a sweet tooth and I cannot resist any type of tart, cake, or biscuit. As you can tell." She gestured to her figure.

"Never deny yourself. I adore your curves."

"I admit, your flattery is doing wonders for my self- confidence. My inner heroine is smitten with you and my inner critic scoffs."

"You can let your inner critic know I will meet the scoundrel at dawn." Sin waved his fit in the air, and she was unable to control the laughter that spilled from her.

"I shall pass that on the next time the ugly head shows itself."

"I have a question for you, Sophie. Your clothing is so flattering and unlike the current fashion. Was that your idea?"

"In fact, it was. I decided to forgo a style that did not suit me and instead chose one that flattered me. I gather it has pleased you?"

"It most certainly has. I do not believe I have ever paid any attention to clothing and the day's fashion until I saw you. Your ingenuity is to be praised."

Sophie was so flattered, both by his comment and the sincerity she heard in his voice. Conversing with Sin was easy, and his proposal was only becoming more attractive. She wanted to ask him more, but they had arrived back at the start of their route. Sin sighed with regret.

"I better get you home before Margot sends out the Royal Guard," he joked as he grazed his knuckles gently across her cheek. A brazen gesture that any passerby may have seen. But she did not care.

"I need to feel your lips on mine. Now."

Chapter Sixteen

Sin could not explain what had come over Sophie, but he was not about to question it. As soon as they entered the carriage, she had pulled the curtains shut and—for lack of a better word—pounced on him. Her kisses were feverish as she ran her hands all over his body. She panted heavily as she broke off the kiss, but he was not done. Sliding his lips down her neck, he kissed and swirled his tongue over silky skin as he used his hands to try to lift her dress. She took her cue from him and moved her hands to his trousers, rubbing his erection. All of a sudden, the carriage came to a halt and Sin pulled the curtain back to see where they were.

Damn! They had arrived at Daniel and Margot's already! "We are here, Sophie, but by God I am ready to take you here and now," he told her gruffly as he looked at her dreamy, soft eyes.

"Perhaps I should apologise for taking such liberties."
"Never. This will just leave me counting the seconds until I see you. What is your schedule before we attend the opera? I don't know if I can wait that long to see you." He realised what a

fool he sounded. It was only three days away, but Sophie had taken control of all his senses.

"I am afraid my schedule is full; I have a luncheon, a dinner party, and errands." She had almost righted herself except for a loose curl he tucked behind her ear.

"I understand. But promise me one thing?" He grasped her jaw so they were gazing directly into each other's eyes. He saw a kaleidoscope of emotions as he searched the jade depths. There was hope, a sprinkle of hesitation, and a dash of fear. He gently brushed his thumb across her soft skin and wished he could convey so much more in that small gesture to persuade her.

"Consider my proposal. I want every free moment with you, not just secret kisses in short carriage rides. I want you to be my wife." He sealed this request with one final searing kiss.

"Where to now, sir?" asked his driver.

Sin was frustrated—sexually and emotionally. A strange combination. He was in no mood to see his father, in no mood to brood back at his rooms at The Albany. He could grab a drink at White's, but that still required a level of socialising.

"Take me to Welles's."

He had recently met with Mr Welles, going through a list of art and objects he wanted to collect. Besides the Grecian pottery, he had not had any other updates. Sin especially wanted to find out how the search went for the Ming bowl. The porcelain beauty with the jade glaze, similar to his jade pin. The same shade of jade that reminded him of Sophie's eyes. While abroad, he had attended a soiree hosted by an

Italian or German aristocrat, the exact details were fuzzy due to his inebriated state. What he did recall was being shown a collection of Ming porcelain. When he had looked into Sophie's eyes he remembered the bowl, and now wanted to buy one as a gift for her. Mr Welles was the best in the business and his eyes had lit up when Sin said that there were no limits on what he was willing to pay. The bowl itself, as he recalled it, was delicate and beautifully rounded—just like Sophie.

By the time he arrived at Welles & Welles, his mood had improved with the hope of good news. The door opened after his first bang of the lion's head knocker and the small man ushered him in.

"How fortuitous you decided to call upon me. I was just writing you a note!" The bespectacled man's excitement meant he had good news.

"Tell me you found the Ming bowl!" Sin matched the man's excitement.

"Yes, My Lord, it will arrive soon. My contact in Italy confirmed that the Count who owned it was looking to part with some of his collection. He was in need of funds, just between you and I, and I negotiated a most reasonable price. There is only one problem." He spoke the last few words nervously.

"And what would that be, Mr Welles?" Sin said as he folded his arms. Surely this problem could be solved.

"After you made your requests, I had another interested person request a Ming bowl with a jade glaze. Usually when this happens, I would arrange a silent auction."

"Who is it?" Sin demanded.

"I am afraid I cannot share that information."

"Well, set up the silent auction," he growled. No wonder the man had been so excited. He had secured the bowl for a reasonable price and would pro!t from a bidding war.

"That was my very intention with the letters I was drafting
—" the sound of the door knocker interrupted Mr Welles.

"I am very sorry, My Lord, but may I please answer that? It
is my next appointment."

Sin sighed but agreed. He was not a brute, and in fairness
he had turned up without an appointment. Mr Welles shuffled
off and Sin looked around the cluttered office. He spied his
name on a note. It appeared Mr Welles had indeed been
writing to him. He saw the piece of paper next to it and
gasped. The mysterious interested party was Sophie! His
annoyance faded as he considered the situation. It was part
humour and part fate, as if this was a sign that Sophie would
marry him. Did he pull out of the auction so she could acquire
it without fuss? Did he let her know he was the other interested party? He had much to ponder and for this he needed a
glass of brandy. He turned to leave and bumped into Mr
Welles.

"For propriety's sake, please have the note delivered. I will
let you know my intentions for the Ming bowl."

Chapter Seventeen

Daniel had decided before the opera that a drink was in order, so Sophie found herself in close proximity to Sin—and Margot and Daniel. His proposal had been all she could think about. It had burrowed deep into her subconscious so that, no matter the task at hand, all thoughts led back to Sin. Sophie knew she would need to face her conflicted emotions and give him an answer, but it felt so soon to even be considering something so...so...forever. Which was the issue. Living with Sin forever

—living in sin, as it were—did not frighten her. Aside from the delicious havoc he wreaked on her body, he touched her mind in a way she never imagined she would experience. The closeness and banter she had always envied between Margot and Daniel was at her fingertips.

But am I ready to give up my newfound independence?

Peeking at him from under her lashes, she watched him throw back his head and laugh at something Daniel said. The deep timbre of the sound reverberated warmly, like that first sip of tea in the morning that settled comfortingly in her belly. She had to fight the urge to reach over and touch him, given their present company. Raising her head, she eyed his handsomeness and caught his smile as he turned to her. The starched white cravat against his tanned face and black-as-sin eyes was dazzling. The pin in his cravat was quite beautiful as well, made of silver and jade. At the thought of jade, she recalled Mr Welles's note that the bowl had been sourced but would require a silent auction. Sin must have noticed her staring at the pin as he removed it and handed it to her.

"It has become my favourite pin; the jade matches your eyes." The slow, sexy smile that unfolded across his face as their fingers made contact made her giggle nervously. *Margot must think I am acting like a silly chit.* She looked up at her friend and, to her surprise, Margot was actually smiling. Sophie had finally told her about Sin's proposal and Margot admitted that perhaps she had been wrong that he would have the intentions of any rakehell. She had not given any opinion on what Sophie's answer should be, but she was at least prepared to offer him a more friendly attitude.

"Sophie had Welles find her Ming bowl in jade, but some other devil is making a bid for it also." Margot informed him.

"Is that right?" Sin asked in a tone that Sophie found a bit too casual.

"Yes, it will be a silent auction. We have been discussing what opening bid Sophie should make."

Daniel clapped his hands to announce it was time to go, which halted any further discussion. Sophie handed Sin his pin, and he barely met her eyes as he fussed over placing it in his cravat. Daniel gave another loud clap with his hands, this time startling Sophie.

"Let the joys of the evening begin!"

Anyone who was anyone was in attendance tonight, and Sophie literally rubbed shoulders making her way to their box. *Il barbiere di Siviglia* had indeed drawn quite the crowd. Taking a seat next to Margot, she admired the view. It was truly magnificent; Daniel was right. Sin and Daniel had yet to join them, so she and Margot indulged in lighthearted gossip as they observed the other guests below. They could not see who was at their left or right, as heavy maroon drapes cordoned off each box.

"I heard *Il barbiere di Siviglia* is quite the comedy," Margot commented.

"Rossini's works are always wonderful. I especially love the string instruments, such lyrical pleasure."

"What is the translation again? Your Italian was always better than mine, Soph."

"It translates to *The Barber of Seville* and was inspired by a play of the same name by Pierre Beaumarchais."

"We come bearing refreshments," Daniel sang, as he and Sin came and sat behind them. Four glasses and two bottles of champagne were followed by one of the wait staff who expertly poured them each a glass. Sophie could not help feeling comforted by the knowledge that Sin was behind her, even if he had acted a little oddly earlier. The proposal was ever constant in her mind and she was warming to it. She could not pretend her objections heavily outweighed this want. If they were already married, when they left later this evening she would not return to a lonely bed, but to his waiting arms. They would talk about their favourite arias and recitatives. She sipped the bubbly liquid and gave Sin one last look, who in turn gave her a cheeky wink, before she turned her attention to the stage.

The overture began and all thoughts $ew from her mind as the sounds of string and woodwind cascaded upon her senses. Sophie closed her eyes and allowed the magic of the musical notes to spread through her being and take her on that sensory journey that can only be experienced at the opera.

Act 1 had finished and the intermission commenced; now the theatre bustled with the sounds of people talking and walking. Sophie gave her head a shake and lamented the assault to her ears after such a glorious first act.

"Sophie, are you with me?" Sin's amused tone broke through her thoughts.

"Sorry, Sin, were you trying to talk to me?" she asked. She turned and was greeted by one of his smouldering smiles. There was something so devilishly handsome about him when his dark eyes glittered with that charming grin.

They were alone. She had not even noticed Margot and Daniel had stepped away.

"I had only asked what your thoughts of the show were so far, though I think your complete rapture is answer enough."

"Rapture is an apt description; it is wonderful. My late husband rarely wanted to attend the kind of performing arts which I thoroughly enjoy."

"Then I will make sure we attend every opera, ballet, and play that is on offer." He gave her a wink.

"You are incorrigible, Sin; I have not yet said yes!" "That is correct, you have not said yes – *yet*."

Sophie rolled her eyes but the knowledge of his blatant want of her was secretly thrilling. She was about to respond, hoping it came out as witty as it sounded in her mind, but he spoke first.

"I want to buy the Ming bowl for you, as a gift."

Sophie was taken aback. Now she felt quite huffy and less than thrilled.

"No, thank you. I want to buy it myself, *for* myself."

"Might it not be very costly though, being a silent auction?"

She felt her eyebrow raise; it felt so high she pictured it almost at her hairline. The audacity!

"I assure you, I will be able to afford it."

To his credit, he looked abashed, but any apology he might have uttered was silenced by Margot and Daniel's return.

Sophie turned around and plastered a false smile on her face till act II began. Once the music started and the singers commenced the dramatic but comedic brouhaha that led to Rosina's marriage, Sophie felt her emotions rise and fall with the tempo of the music. To take a word from Margot's unladylike vocabulary, Sinclair Montgomery was a complete addle pate!

Chapter Eighteen

Sin sat in the study of the Montgomery townhouse and folded the note he had just written. He toyed with writing another note, but now considered delivering the words orally. He sighed as he fingered the paper in his hands. It was eight o'clock in the morning, too early for a drink, but he needed something to numb his senses. Sin knew he had uttered the wrong words the previous evening as soon as they left his mouth. He had not meant to imply she could not afford to buy the bowl. Sophie's cold tone still echoed in his mind. His independent, saucy, clever, luscious Sophie – his Goddess. He had attempted to break down her walls so she would say yes to his proposal but instead he had added another layer to penetrate. He groaned out loud and placed his forehead on the desk. It was not being a jealous fool that ruined things, it was being a presumptuous fool.

"Why am I such a complete fool?"

"Pardon me, My Lord. I believe you called for me?"

Sin glanced up at an uncomfortable-looking Jack, who had evidently witnessed his descent into this pathetic and rueful state. He had called for him to deliver a letter to Mr Welles, to advise him that he no longer had an interest in the Ming bowl. He gave Jack the letter and instructions and went back to his brooding.

"Sinclair, what are you doing awake at this early hour?" He heard his father's voice.

"I am lamenting, Father, for I have been a fool."

He took a seat in front of Sin and smiled. "Does this involve the mysterious woman you find yourself infatuated with?"

Sin nodded. "You know, when I came home at your behest I had no interest in settling down. But before I even arrived home, I caught sight of this woman and I have fallen hard for her. Harder than I even knew was possible."

"Any woman to bring you to your knees must be quite a woman indeed. When do I get to meet her?"

"Well, that is the problem. I fear I offended her last evening, and she isn't the type for whom flowers and a sorry will do. Worse than that, I had asked her to marry and she was thinking it over. I apologise for not letting you know sooner that I had proposed to someone."

His father waved him off. "Not at all. You know I do not like to meddle. All I want for you is to be happy. That was all I wanted for your brother as well. What any good parent should want. I know I harp on about your duty to the family name and that stems from pride. We are Montgomerys! But with your brother and now with you, a"airs of the heart will be your choice."

Sin felt a rush of affection for his father; he was a good man. Whenever they spoke of Andrew's passing it helped the continuous healing that is grief.

"Anyhow, Sinclair, tell me more about this woman and let's see how you can earn back her good graces."

Returning his father's grin, he threw up his hands.

"Her name is Sophie Westcott. She is widowed and best

friends with Daniel's wife. She is clever and cultured; we share a passion for art and artefacts. Her hair is a fiery ginger that sets off her jade green eyes. And her body is all soft, round curves. You would think she is a Greco-Roman statue. You were right; she has a fierce independence that I find very desirable."

He realised he sounded like a love-struck chit, but he didn't care.

"She sounds wonderful, Sinclair. From what you tell me, I think you need to speak with her in person and clear up whatever this misunderstanding is."

Sin banged the desk with his hands and rose to his feet. "You are absolutely correct! I am going to call on her now and see if we cannot sort this out. And if we can, I am going to spirit her off to Gretna Green lest I put my foot in it again!".

"Off you go then, my boy."

Sin did not bother with a carriage and saddled a horse in order to get there as quickly as possible. Daniel's butler lifted his eyebrows ever so slightly in surprise when he opened the door to Sin and a horse.

"Sorry for the early hour, good man, but I must speak with Her Grace. Have a stableboy take care of my horse." He had barely remembered she was the widow of a Duke.

"Is that you I hear, Sin?" said Daniel from behind the butler.

"Yes, it is me, I must speak with Sophie." He handed the reins to the butler and stepped inside.

"Make yourself comfortable in the drawing room. She is probably still asleep, Margot is."

Daniel asked the housekeeper to check on Sophie and advise her that Sin was here. They sat in the drawing room and Daniel poured them each a cup of strongly brewed tea.

"So what is this all about? Our Sophie has certainly gotten under your skin, hasn't she?" Daniel tried to hide his smile behind his teacup, but Sin saw the corners of his eyes crinkle.

"Did Margot tell you that I asked Sophie to marry me? I gather Sophie informed her."

"Yes, she told me last night after I asked an incessant number of questions as to the tension between you and Sophie."

"In these few short weeks, I have fallen utterly and completely in love with her and I want to marry her."

The sound of a throat being cleared made him turn his head and he felt his cheeks flame. It was Sophie.

"Ah, I will give you two some privacy," Daniel said as he made a hasty exit.

"Sophie, I hope I did not wake you?" She looked a vision in a white day dress with accents of green that complimented her colouring.

"No, I have been up for a while. I did not sleep very well." Her tone was not warm but neither was it cold. She sounded weary? Curious?

Do I acknowledge what she just overheard now or after my speech?

"Sophie, first and foremost, I want to discuss what happened last night."

Chapter Nineteen

Sophie was working so very hard to compose herself. A smile threatened to break free as she watched this dashing supposed rake squirm in his chair after she overheard him declare his love. She had decided she wanted to speak with him as well. There was something special between them and she was not ready to cry quits over what she hoped was only a poor choice of words. If it wasn't, she intended to make it clear that it would be the first and last time he challenged her independence—especially if she was to consider marriage. After her inner heroine and inner critic battled all night, she decided she wanted it all and she would have it all. A life where she made her own decisions alongside a husband who made her toes curl. A life where she was an equal partner with whom to talk of any topic and tackle any issue. She would not settle for less. Sitting up straight and plastering a serious expression on her face, she gave him a nod.

"I am listening, Sin."

"After that first night we met, I asked Mr Welles to source the Ming bowl. I wanted to gift you a precious piece of art that reminded me of you. When I was last there, he gave me the good news that he had found it but advised me there was another person interested. He would not tell me who it was. When he stepped out of his office, I unscrupulously spied a note with your name on his desk and realised you were that other person. It was never my intention to suggest I purchase it because you could not afford it, I just wanted to gift it to you. I sent him a note this morning withdrawing from the silent auction. You must know I find your independence attractive. I adore all the things that make you so uniquely you. I had no plans for marriage until I set my eyes upon you, and if you give me a chance I will worship you like the Goddess you are."

The earnestness in his voice rang true, as did the genuine warmth shining in his dark eyes. Sophie felt her own eyes moisten at his heartfelt speech. Sin knelt down in front of where she sat and grabbed her hands, encapsulating them in his much larger ones.

"I hope those tears welling are those of happiness?" he murmured as he searched her face.

"They are indeed. I suspected there was more to the Ming bowl when you acted oddly as soon it was mentioned yesterday. I very much appreciate your intentions and now know you meant no insult. What I need you to understand is what the bowl represents—it is the first thing of value and personal sentiment I am buying for myself. I have come to value who I am. I now know who I am. Not someone's daughter or someone's wife. If I marry again, I want a partner, a friend, a lover. I want it all." Her voice was husky, full of emotion, but she made sure she had gotten the most important words out.

Now, she carefully searched his eyes for any sign of discontent at what she told him, but thankfully all she saw was admiration.

"Sophie, I have no desire for a loveless marriage or for a tyrannical rule over our lives. That is for weak, small-minded men. I want what you want, and I never knew I wanted it till I met you. I do have one request though."

"Yes?"

"Well, a request and a question. I request that you allow me to spoil you now and then with surprises and gifts. And my question is—will you marry me?"

"I agree to be spoiled unless I have already voiced my own intentions, but I won't deny the thrill it gives me to be so cherished by you." She pulled her hands out of his grip to cup his face and leaned close so their noses touched. "And I will be honoured to be your wife, Sinclair Montgomery." She kissed his full lips softly to seal her answer.

Sin pulled them both to their feet, placing one arm around her waist and the other at her nape and dipped her slightly with his lips still pressed to hers. He coaxed open her lips with a sweep of his tongue and kissed her slowly but fiercely, setting her aflame right to the core with the erotic promise of their future. Sophie splayed her hands across his broad chest, clutching at his shirt as her legs started to turn to mush.

"Sophie, I am tempted to take you right here and now," he panted against her mouth as he pulled them both upright. Their chests were still pressed against each other, both their hearts pounding wildly.

"Ahem. Let us make haste to Gretna Green to get you lovebirds wedded and bedded?" Daniel said in an amused tone.

Sophie jumped at the intrusion and turned to find a smiling Daniel and Margot watching them.

"That sounds like a fantastic idea, Daniel. Ready yourselves and meet me down the road at mine. I will invite my father and get ready." Sin halted and turned to Sophie. "If that is fine with you, Sophie?" He looked stricken that he had not asked her already.

"Of course. This is what I want, to be wedded so we can start our lives together. In this, you and I are on the same page, my darling," she said as she kissed him. "Before we go, I will write to Mr Welles and make an offer on the Ming bowl."

Their little group scattered and Sophie took a moment of silence back in her room to reflect on all that had just taken place. Looking at herself in the mirror, she ran her hands over her body. She started at her breasts, swept to the dips at her waist and across her derrière. She felt each bump, angle, and lump and sighed happily. In a short few weeks, she had embraced her true self, her wants and needs, and her curves. She had shaken herself free of the status quo, dressing for flattering suitability and not ill-fitting trends. She knew the sensual touch of a man and the climactic heights her body could soar to. She moved to find her stationery, taking her first step towards the successful purchase of a piece of history. From here on out, she would live life unapologetically, boldly, and curvaceously with a surname she chose—she was Sophie Montgomery. And she chose Sin.

They travelled for hours with minimal stops; she and Sin were so eager to reach that blacksmith's anvil. They had taken two carriages, swapping company at each stop. When Sophie found herself with Sin's father she was a little nervous, but then he smiled that charming Montgomery smile and she instantly felt at ease.

"I am so delighted to meet you, Sophie. The first time Sinclair spoke of you, I had a feeling you would become my daughter-in-law."

"I was unsure how much you knew of me before this. I am pleased to know that not only was I not a surprise, but that he talked of me." She blushed and felt silly.

"Do not feel embarrassed. Love is grand and it is a joy to be around. My son tells me you are also a lover of the arts. My boys grew up with Montgomery artefacts that date back to William the Conqueror and they were never impressed by them, so I am excited to share them with you."

Sophie tensed at the word 'love.' She knew that that was what she was feeling but could not bring herself to yet say it. In her experience, marriage and love did not go hand in hand. But she refused to allow the past to ruin her present.

"I would be delighted! It thrills me to know I will be in a family with such rich history."

"And better yet, if it interests you, many pieces need to be catalogued as they have not been tended to for an age."

Now this truly excited Sophie.

"That is the most wonderful wedding present I could ever expect," Sophie exclaimed. "Now tell me about Sin when he was young. I am certain he got up to all kinds of mischief."

"Luckily, we have a ways to go. That will give me enough time to cover his childhood before we move into his years at Eton."

Chapter Twenty

And just as quick as the strike of the anvil, they were married. Sin would be the first to admit that he was feeling very much the blushing bride, besotted as he was with his wife. He recalled the huskiness of her voice as she said yes to becoming his bride. Her words were sure and spoken without falter as she held his gaze. Those tiny details spoke volumes to him; they told him she was making the decision confidently and without doubts.

Sophie had just finished dressing and was ready to go downstairs to meet his father, Margot, and Daniel for a celebratory evening meal. She hummed softly to herself as he walked over and embraced her from behind.

"I adore you, Sophie. I look at you and wonder at how unbelievably fortuitous it was that I laid my eyes on you the very first day I returned home. Not a single moment was wasted on not being enthralled by you."

"Sin, that is incredibly touching. I want to pinch myself as a reminder that this is real. These few weeks you have showered me with more love than I received in all the years of my first marriage."

"There is a simple reason for that."

"Oh. Do tell?" she teased, as she turned around to give him a sweet kiss.

"I fell in lust the moment I laid my eyes on you but when you stood by that Botticelli —beautiful and challenging my thoughts—I am adamant that is the moment when I fell in love with you. Even if I did not know it at the time."

Tears welled in her eyes. She did not respond with words but captured his mouth in a searing kiss. He returned it ardently, the emotion between them only intensifying the moment.

He felt her groan in his mouth, the vibration a gentle purr as she placed her hands at the back of his head and pulled him in closer. Unable to restrain himself, he roughly grabbed at the flesh of her curves. He loved how her breast spilled over his hand and the plumpness of her buttocks.

"Sin, you are turning me into a wild woman," she panted hotly into the curve of his neck as she ground against him. Their clothes only added to the friction between them. He was rock hard again, straining against his trousers. He lifted her up and clutched those perfectly rounded cheeks so he could rub his cock against her mound. But it was not enough.

"I am not letting you leave until I bury myself inside you again."

She nodded wordlessly, her eyes hazed with lust, and lifted up her skirts. Freeing himself, his trousers dropped to his ankles, and he guided her backwards so she was against a wall. He hoisted her up and she immediately raised her legs.

"That's right my gorgeous Goddess, wrap those thighs around me."

He sank into her with a groan. There was no finesse in his movement, just purpose. A need to feel her heat pulsating around him. They were at a perfect angle where he knew he was hitting her sweet spot, feeling her legs tremble. With each thrust, she let out a gasp that drove him harder and harder until he exploded inside her, roaring his satisfaction.

"Sin, hush or else everyone will know what we just did," she gasped, gripping him tightly as her own release shuddered throughout her body.

"I cannot help it! You may be a Goddess, but you are turning me into a beast!"

"A sinful beast that I love with every fibre of my being."

"Is that so? More than the Ming bowl?" he teased. The words slowly sank in.

She loves me!

"Hmm, that is a tough choice. You know how much I adore the bowl," she said between giggles.

Her face was flushed with a happiness he hoped to see every day.

"What is your inner heroine telling your inner critic at this very moment?"

She crinkled her nose in concentration, and he pressed a kiss to her freckles.

"It is telling me that I was right in following my heart; from designing the dresses I wanted to wear, to pursuing my passion for the arts that bring me joy, to finding a man that made me feel desired just as I am. And I am a Goddess."

Author's Note for you, wonderful Reader

In honour of releasing His Regency Goddess as an audiobook and now in paperback, this updated manuscript replaces the current ebook but never fear the story remains exactly the same! Following on your will see more of my works, released & upcoming!

At the beginning of 2024 a dear author friend put out feelers for someone to take her spot in a historical romance collaboration promoting 'body positivity'. I wanted to put my hand up but realised I had no works in progress around this. Within a couple of days, the characters of Sophie & Sin came to me, and a plot started to form, and I put my hand up. The title 'His Regency Goddess' came to me as soon as I decided to draw inspiration from Botticelli's 'The Birth of Venus. And from there it snowballed – in the best of ways! By June, my novella was complete including two beta reads, line editing and proofreading. A great of example of what can happen when you commit your all to a goal.

My motivation to promote body positivity and the voluptuous female figure in all its glory was partly personal. Reflecting on my younger years, they were filled with warped expectations of what I wanted to see in the mirror. Which still sneakily appears on a dark day. Majority of my days however, I wake up loving and appreciating my body. Curves, dimples, rolls and all! So, when I wrote this story, Sophie's voice teetered on the edge of self-acceptance and owning her curvaceous beauty. Not one of struggle. And who wouldn't want their very own Sin to worship them from head to toe!

If you take anything away from this story – love yourself for all the things that make you unique and inherently you.

Steffy Smith xxx

About the Author

About the Author

Steffy is forever reading, forever dreaming. And mainly, forever wishing she was dancing at a Regency Ball, drinking *uisge beatha* in a medieval Scottish keep, navigating a Norman-Saxon romance, or riding up on horseback into a Western town.

Follow her writing journey, as one by one these stories will unfold. To be kept informed of new releases, updates, and most importantly to connect with any feedback or reviews, please sign up to her newsletter at www.steffysmithbooks.com.

Also by Steffy Smith

An English Garden

(Georgian England)

A Marquess of Roses

An Earl of Bluebells

*A Viscount of Lavender (coming 2027)**

*A Baron of Thistles (coming 2027)**

Highland Hearts

(Medieval Scotland)

The Bonniest Lass in Scotland

Highland Heartbreaker

*Book III (coming 2027)**

Curves&Cravats

(Regency England)

His Regency Goddess

Romancing the Rake Anthology

The Widow Reforms A Rake

(Regency England Short)

Lore & Love Trilogy

(Viking Age)

Her Viking Saviour

*Spring Maiden (coming 2026)**

*Viking in Love (coming 2027)**

Suffragette Uprising

Natural Impatience & Righteous Indignation (Coming 2026)

Regency Runaway Brides

Regina is Out of Luck (coming 2026)

Wicked Widows League

The Widow Takes a Lover (coming 2026)

**Publication year subject to change.*

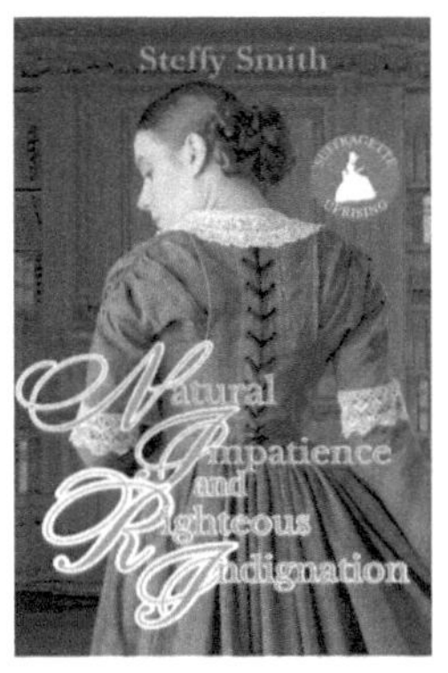

Coming in 2026

Coming in 2026

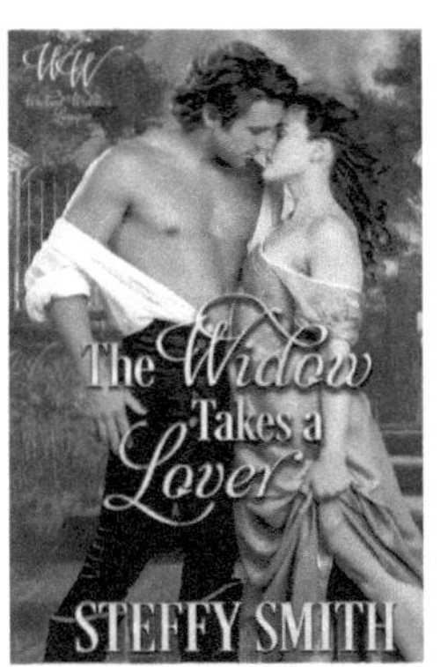

Coming in 2026

A

Marquess
of Roses

An English Garden

STEFFY SMITH

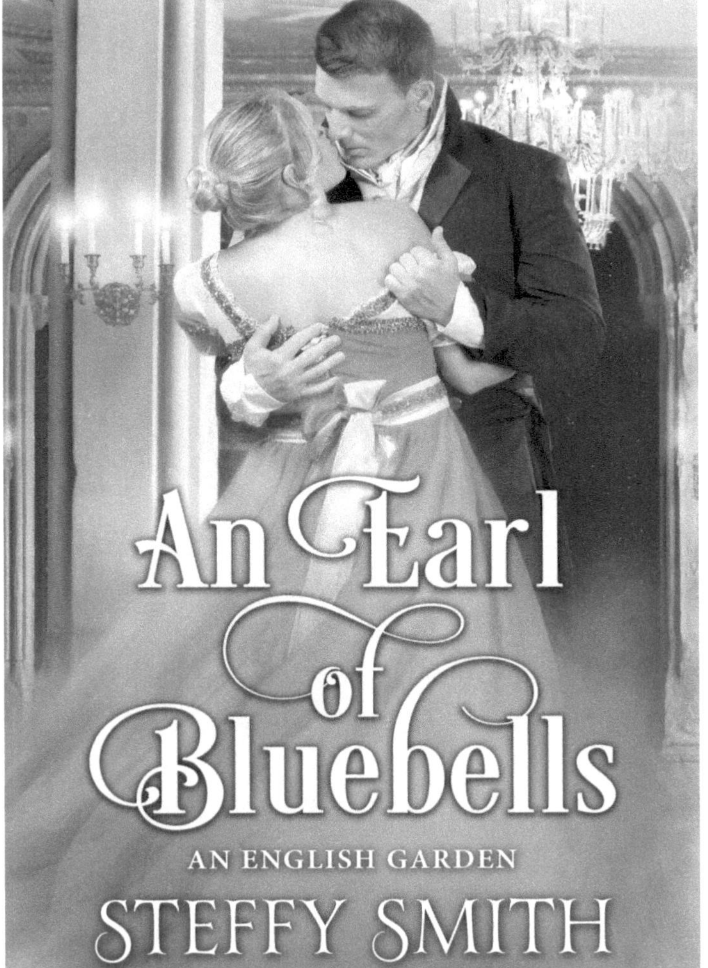
An Earl
of
Bluebells
AN ENGLISH GARDEN
STEFFY SMITH

The
Bonniest
Lass In
Scotland
HIGHLAND HEARTS BOOK ONE
STEFFY SMITH

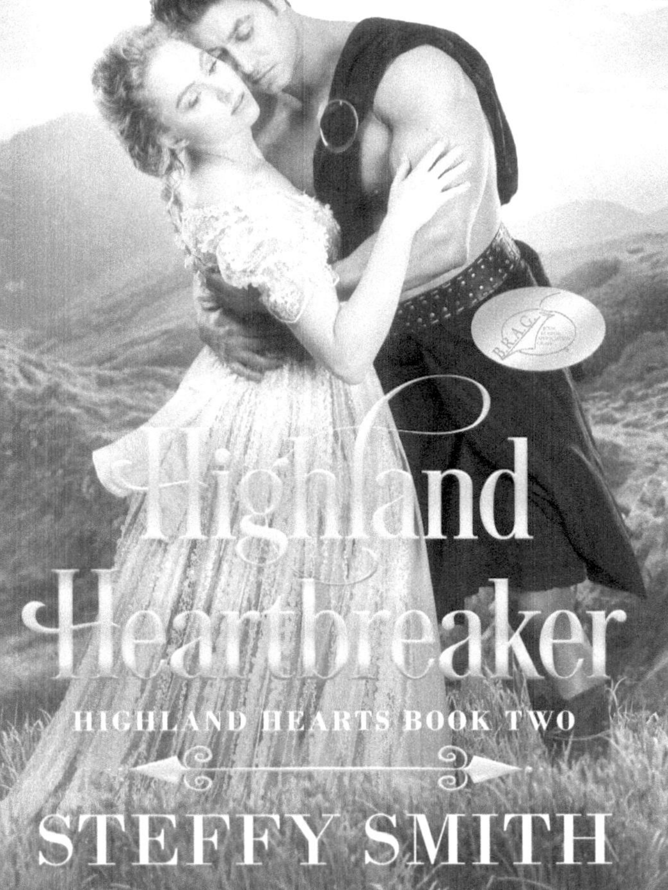

Highland
Heartbreaker
HIGHLAND HEARTS BOOK TWO
STEFFY SMITH

Lore
&
Love
Trilogy
Book I
Her Viking Saviour
STEFFY SMITH

STEFFY SMITH

The Widow Reforms A Rake

A Historical Short

WD
WAYWARD DUKES
The Governess
Teaches
A Duke
STEFFY SMITH

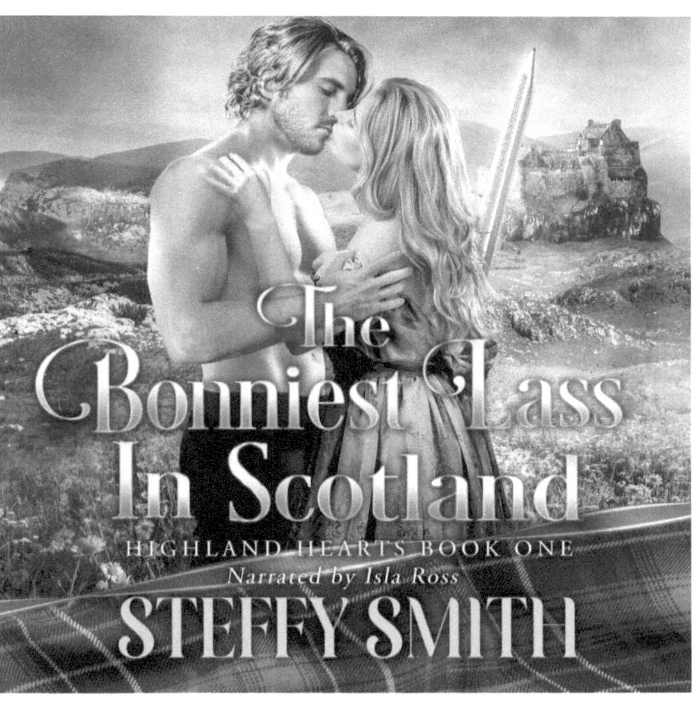
The Bonniest Lass In Scotland
HIGHLAND HEARTS BOOK ONE
Narrated by Isla Ross
STEFFY SMITH

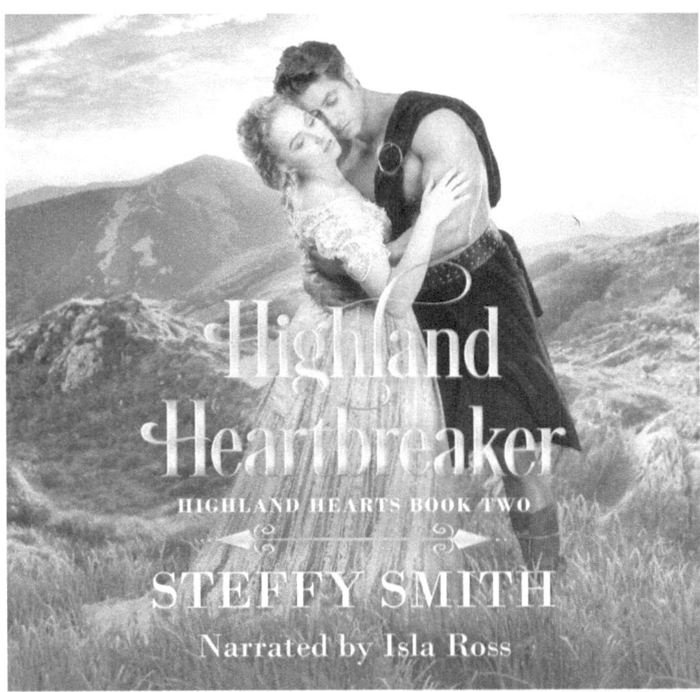

Highland
Heartbreaker
HIGHLAND HEARTS BOOK TWO
STEFFY SMITH
Narrated by Isla Ross

CURVES & CRAVATS
His
Regency
Goddess
STEFFY SMITH
NARRATED BY ISLA ROSS